A Witness of Waxwings invites us into worlds of shifting time and identities, where brutal reality is often witnessed through a liminal lens. Within these stories are shifts of light, perception, slips into other realms, where people are inhabited by birds, selkies and sprites. There are ghosts in the ocean, faces in the wake. Alison Lock's fictional world is a route map to unexplored mindscapes.

❧

Alison Lock is a poet and author living in the Pennines of West Yorkshire. Her short stories often explore the liminal spaces of our relationship with the natural world, and her writing is inspired by the landscape of the moors, the rivers, and the sea. Her readings have taken her from Scotland to Cornwall, and Vienna. As well as writing and tutoring Life Writing courses, she has found joy in singing with local acapella groups and choirs.

www.alisonlock.com

A truly accomplished writer whose sparkling prose leads you gently away from your comfort zones. What lies within Alison Lock's fictional world is a route map to unexplored mindscapes.

Jose Varghese, Editor, *Lakeview International Review*

Alison's stories of transformation sparkle with originality and are alive with sensual detail.

Michael Stewart, author of *Ill Will*

Alison Lock has a gift for making the ordinary extraordinary and the mundane remarkable. Her prose is exquisite, and as well-crafted and lyrical as ever.

Teika Bellamy, Editor and Publisher

Alison Lock writes with delicacy about brutality, with the eye of truth turned equally on reality and fantasy. She glances and looks away, her retinal after-images caught on the page.

Cherry Potts, Arachne Press

Also by Alison Lock

Poetry
A Slither of Air (Indigo Dreams Publishing, 2011)
Beyond Wings (Indigo Dreams Publishing, 2015)
Revealing the Odour of Earth (Calder Valley Poetry, 2017)

Novella
Maysun and the Wingfish (Mother's Milk Books, 2016)

Short Stories
Above the Parapet (Indigo Dreams Publishing, 2013)

A Witness
of Waxwings

ALISON LOCK

Cultured Llama Publishing

First published in 2017 by
Cultured Llama Publishing
www.culturedllama.co.uk

ISBN 978-0-9957381-5-7

Printed in Great Britain by Lightning Source UK Ltd

Cover illustration and design: Mark Holihan
Author photo: Jean Bashford

Contents

Wink

Our business is with mats and blocks on a carpet patterned with swirls of paisley-seeds, like haemoglobin curls. We are kept warm by the gas heater, the constant swish of pump and burn gives us a rhythm as we, cell by cell, fill the room.

We hold onto the backs of chairs. They creak as if to gird their ribs for each lifting limb, while we create non-human shapes that bend, concave, convex.

On the wall is a portrait of a woman. Her face is so faint, almost pellucid, but shining through a mist of dust and time. She seems unperturbed by our wavering arms; our shadows are crossing the rectangle of her confined world.

With one foot against our inner thighs, we wobble, our hands rising in prayer-like clasp above our heads, grasping for the point of balance until, eventually, we all describe our upturned hearts.

The final minutes are for restful meditation: skulls

cradled, blankets folded over bodies, tucked under feet. A candle sputters with golden light, and incense hangs in a silent fug.

The woman of the portrait gazes out, her inert grace contained within the perfect symmetry of the gilded frame. We listen to the spoken parts: the solar plexus, throat and heart; the sensing of each chakra vibrating with our ohms. The inner eye has opened.

I see her wink.

Into the Blue

A bee is trapped behind the curtains – its silhouette circles the head of a printed flower. Edith pulls her arm free of the tightly tucked sheet and watches the hand rising. The skin on the wrist and hand is loose, mottled, the blue veins twisted, weaving around the bones. It is the hand of one who is old, and she does not, will not recognise it. A sound rises in her throat, but it fades before the word, the question reaches her lips. She wonders how she became tethered to this ancient husk.

Against the far wall is a wardrobe. One of its veneered doors is ajar, breaking the symmetry. Edith stretches forward to catch hold of the hanger, the wooden one, the one with the bevelled edges, its curved nape embossed with a bird in flight. Draped across its breadth is the blue organza dress.

Mother, the seamstress, the worker of miracles, is watched by the young Edith. She is leaning over yards of blue material, folding and unfolding, fitting the pattern

3

with precision, wasting nothing. She pushes in the pins, cuts through the layers of cloth and tracing paper with heavy tailoring scissors. Her tacking is neat; every stitch held up to the light, her spectacles balanced on the edge of her nose catching the flash of the silver thimble in their frame with each push of the needle.

Edith looks back to the bed. The old woman is still there, her hand raised as if frozen. Tight as swaddling, the sheets are tucked in around her as if she is mummified. Somewhere on the cusp of sleep and dream, she is slipping through doorways, sidling along high-walled alleyways. She turns a corner, but she is looking straight into a mirror – the wardrobe mirror. She unrolls the paper curlers, revealing springs of auburn hair. She pulls and pats at the coiled slivers.

She is wearing the blue dress, and she admires the tailored lines, how it hugs her body. She runs her hands over the curve of her breasts and the arc of her hipbones, noting how the hem falls discreetly over her knees. Turning, side to the glass, she follows the contours of her calves; below are her feet in their peep-toe shoes. She feels them pinching at the heels; the first sign of a blister.

She is walking through the front door of the terraced house and onto the street, where the pavement is bleached by the sun. It is the bone end of summer, and though barely dusk, the heat scorches the air. Flecks of mica flash from the paving slabs; tiny fragments of quartz have become sprinklings of diamonds beneath her feet. She walks past the end of the terrace where the road broadens into an avenue. A handbag hangs from a chain on her arm. Inside, slipped into a silk-lined pocket is the invitation. *You are invited to join us for the celebration of the engagement...*

Everyone knows it is a perfect match; the families are united by decades of picnics and Sunday high teas. She was there as they skipped from one joyous reunion to the next: Edith the companion, the faithful friend, watching from the sidelines as they gushed in and out of her simple life on a festive tide.

But these are faint images, remainders, that ebb away before she can study them. She feels for the blue dress, clutching at the loose material over her body, but it is a different body, one that aches, bony and bruised. The cloth is merely a counterpane. The room echoes as she grasps at sounds, whispers – until a single voice cuts through.

'Edith, Edith. Are you awake, dear? It's a lovely day. Let's go into the garden.'

Her hand is stroked, with warmth – by one who knows that old skin feels more keenly, that kind strokes ease more than words. A gown is held out for her. It is blue – but this is no party dress, merely a pilled dressing gown. As she is lowered into the seat beside the bed, the light catches the chrome of its wheels.

Outside, a blackbird is jabbing at the lawn, catching the dew. The sun has yet to reach the pond where the blue-tailed damselflies hover and flit, zipping from one reed to the next. The lawn is a soft length of green for the stars of daisies.

'He loves me; he loves me not. He loves me, he loves me not.' Edith is chanting.

'Who loves you, Edith?'

'He loves me...'

Her eyes close around the imprint of the sun. She listens to the sparrows as they chatter around the bird table, their wings fluttering as they dip and hover on the edge, pecking at the seed.

The chatter stops, and she feels a breeze lifting her hair at the nape of her neck. Edith's eyes are open. A flock of starlings has arrived.

'He loves me not!'

The sky is filling with dark clouds, and cold air rushes by as she is taken back to the room with the wardrobe. But something is missing – from the bed, from the pillow. It is always there. The – but she cannot remember the word. A tiny lady not made of flesh. Her favourite, her best – doll, yes, that is it. Her doll is missing. So grand in her velvet gown; Princess has always graced the throne of Edith's pillow. Never the kind of doll to be wheeled along the street in a pram, to be poked and smudged by the fingers of others jealous of her beauty. Even Edith's sister must not touch.

Outside, the gutters are filling as thunder rolls, exploding in bursts of rain. But Edith is indoors, pushing a wheeled frame before her. Someone is beside her, encouraging. One step at a time, no need to rush, and she is through into a vast lounge.

'Hello, Edith.'

'How lovely!' Edith exclaims.

'So,' the face looks surprised. 'You know who I am today?' The visitor has her hand on Edith's arm.

'I have searched everywhere, but...' the woman's voice is faltering.

Edith pats the hand, reassuring.

'Edith. There is no trace. I am so sorry.'

The woman presses a photograph into Edith's hand. It is black and white, and the young woman in the picture is wearing a hat that is pulled down over her head. Behind her is a wall of brick and the corner of a sash window. Her face is visible beneath the brim, distinct in the glare of the flashlight. The eyes hold both pride and fear. She is holding a baby, a bonny baby. Edith stares. A moment of recognition. A fading smile.

The wide eyes, the tight lips are like those of her mother. The mouth, slightly pursed, like when holding the pins.

'Keep still, Edie, it's hard enough without you wriggling.'

Edith is standing on a chair; Mother is tutting and pulling at the bottom edge of the dress.

'I won't be able to let it out any more, you know.'

'Are you nearly finished?'

Edith is impatient. The last stitch is done, but Mother does not let go of the folds of material.

'I saw him today,' Mother says. 'Frank...'

Her voice is hesitant, stilted, perhaps because of the pins, or maybe it is because she has guessed.

Frank's face flashes in front of Edith. She can see the line of his jaw, the tensed muscle, the flicker below the cheekbone. Nauseous, she reels.

Later, she sees him in the queue at the cinema. He is with Lucy. They are standing under the bright lights of the box office, their pale faces distorted in the glass, enlarged. His arm is around her shoulder, the same arm that was propped against the mantelpiece that evening, the evening of the engagement party when the room pulsed, spinning with laughter, conversation, the clink of glasses, the thrum of music.

The liquid in Frank's glass is ochre, and the beads around Lucy's neck are white; her neck is flushed. Lucy is pulling at his hand, trying to persuade him to dance, but he will not. His eyes are bright but restless, giving him an untethered look. The band starts to play. It is a number that everyone recognises; slow at first and then the music quickens. The floor fills with dancing couples. Lucy turns away; another man invites her to dance, and as she spins in his arms her laughter rips across the room.

'Well, well. If it's not our little Edie.' Frank's face is blocking Edith's view; his breath is stifling.

'Congratulations, Frank,' Edith says, 'to you both, of course.'

He does not reply. Nor does he break eye contact.

'I need some fresh air,' he says. 'Will you join me?'

She faces the black shadows of the garden as she leans on the railings of the veranda.

'You're not shy, are you?' Frank asks.

She remembers that she is with the boy who used to

live here, the boy who liked to play hide-and-seek, to jump out at her and Josephine, pointing at them, making fun of their screams. But now he is a man, and she is with him on the veranda.

'Edie,' he croons.

His voice is strange. Edith cannot see his face because he is behind her, too close. He has one hand on either side, pressing her into the rails. His body is firm against hers, so she is unable to turn around.

'I think we should go back inside,' she says.

She remains still, but she knows he is not listening. His breath is sickly sweet. She is wedged between his body and the railings. She feels the weight of muscle and bone. She is about to say that she will scream, but before she can he has covered her mouth with one hand and he is biting at the dress, pulling it away from her shoulders. The more she struggles, the more he continues, laughing as if they are playing a game. Perhaps he will claim at any moment that he is only pretending, and she will feel silly for making a fuss. She holds her breath and hears the music coming from inside, so close.

It is a waltz. Edith is counting the beats in her head... one, two, three...

The blue dress tears as it is pulled up as he is pushing into her, hurting her. She cries out, but the hand over her mouth muffles the sound. She knows that no one can hear her now; the ears of the night are deaf.

The pain stops as the pressure against her is released, and she is holding onto the cold rail as if she will never let it go. The music becomes louder, of a sudden, for the moment between the door opening and the door shutting. Edith is alone, shivering, and below her, through the railings, is a long drop to where the ground is black. She leans forward and vomits.

She will tell them; let them know what he has done, she will raise the alarm. They will see the blood on her shoes.

They will believe her. They must do.

As she goes through the door, a glass flute is pressed into her hand and everyone in the room is standing. No one sees her, as all eyes look towards Frank and Lucy.

'Raise your glass for a toast to the lovely couple!'

Everyone lifts their glasses, and their goodwill fills the room. Edith sways.

'Rock-a-bye baby on the tree top,' Edith sings.

She clutches a pillow, staring into the crook of her arm, rocking forward and back. The woman is there again with her soft hands on Edith's cold bones. She is gently pulling at the pillow, and Edith releases it. She does not resist. The photograph is floating in the air, spinning like a broken wing, skimming the ground before it stops at Edith's feet.

A spoon dips into the soup. Edith stops it with her tongue, not allowing it to enter her mouth. The soup has the odour of salt and earth and blood. The wind flutes through the loose pane of the window. The bee has gone, and the curtains are billowing.

Her sister was the naughty one, always up to mischief, hiding in the bay of the window, legs tucked up, behind the green velvet curtain. They are in the parlour and Mother is speaking in a half-whisper, urgently, kneading her hands.

'Are you absolutely sure?'

'Yes,' Edith says.

A crash is followed by a shattering onto the stone tiles. The beautiful doll, the Princess, is face down on the floor, the fine porcelain face smashed, a single eye flickers on a spring in the fractured socket. Her sister has fled.

The rain has arrived, and water fills the runnels and gutters, gathering around the blocked drains. It plashes the ground, filling and rising with each breath. Edith dips her head down, presses her palms together and pushes her arms up, out, back to her sides, up and out again. She is swimming.

The bathing house is empty. The blue and white tiles glisten as the sun's rays penetrate the glass-domed roof, filtering through the deep water, reflecting tiny windows of light. The only shadow is from a bird perched high on the roof, and, as it takes off, its wings spread in flight and feathered shadows disperse as Edith glides through the blue of the pool. Her body floats easily. She has no aches, no pain. The weight of her womb no longer drags, and as she turns onto her back, her belly rises like a half moon. She is neither flying nor swimming – her baby swims free.

Rip Tide

Nothing can stop the swell of the tide; nipping in, lingering, snatching at ankles. And all with a speed of return that can outpace the swiftest runner. Even the gulls are made clumsy, buffeted by the wind aroused by the swirling sea. The sun is past its zenith but still retains its heat – so much so that one could easily be fooled by the placid flicker of yellow light and the gentle shush of the swaying tide.

Three children are building a castle on the hard sand below the tideline. It is a tumble of turrets and channels and a moat – the familiar outline of a medieval fortification. They pant and puff as they shovel and pat down the soft grains into their buckets, releasing them with a tap on the upturned mould.

Pippa, the youngest, is planting a garden of shells around the edges: cockles and tiny conches hem the raised keep. Her feet stray too close to the edge of the moat, and it happens: the fragile sides crumble.

'Watch out, clumsy!', Alfie shouts.

Panicked, Pippa slips further into the moat, stumbling against the castle, breaking down the walls.

'Go away, Pippa.' Laura – older sister – is exasperated. 'Just go back to Mum and Greg.'

'But I want to stay here...' Pippa's bottom lip is quivering.

'We don't want you here anymore,' Alfie says. 'You're spoiling everything.'

'Leave her alone.' Laura won't have anyone else talking to her little sister in that way.

Tears are now falling from Pippa's cheeks.

'She's spoilt.' Alfie kicks at a bucket and shoves his spade into the crushed side of the castle.

There's something spiteful about the way the metal edge cuts into the sand. 'She's a cry baby,' he says. 'My dad says so.'

'Well, he's not her dad,' Laura says, her face reddening. 'Anyway, he can't say that.'

A gull screams and dives onto the ground where the tiny oyster shells lie in the pattern of a star. After stabbing at a piece of shell with its beak, finding that the shiny white thing is not the piece of food he had hoped for, the gull flies off inland, one eye tilted towards the ground. Further up the beach is a scattering of human beings, like glistening slicks on the sand.

Julie, the girls' mother, is among them. As she rolls onto her front, a sprinkling of sand sticks to her basted body. She is infuriated with Greg as she thinks about him back at the hotel where the Wi-Fi keeps him on the end of its invisible leash, dealing with his business, just like every other morning that week. He will be controlling his world with his annoying voice: the voice that only a year ago filled her with admiration and, she has to admit, desire.

Julie turns her head towards the shoreline. It's quite a way to where the children are building their castle, but she can make out their shapes, and deduces from the way they are that they're OK. Laura would let her know if anything was wrong. She can make out the outline of Greg's son standing on the top of a mound. She has tried so hard with Alfie, but his tiresome habit of teasing the girls is very irritating. She has tried to persuade her daughters that there are advantages to having an older brother, and that the five of them can be a complete and happy family. Greg is very supportive – he's even paid for Pippa to be taken to a counsellor to try to resolve her difficulties with Alfie. He's often buying new toys, paying for activities – he is very kind in that way.

At times Julie is filled with grief, not over death, although that is just how it feels – times of weeping, times of anger, times of deep sadness. The sense of fracture that she has felt since the split up with Paul feeds into her determination to make it work this time. She knows that the odds are stacked against 'blended families', but she is determined it will work for them, for her girls, for the five of them as a new family. It's just that sometimes it feels as if there are too many emotions, too many needs. And sometimes she wishes time would pass – that ten years would slip by and all this was behind them. But then she feels guilty for wishing her children's childhoods away.

The flesh of Julie's back tingles as her spine, her neck and shoulders, gently roast in the sun. She flicks away the grains of sand that have encroached onto the towel. But first, she will write a postcard to her parents. At least she does not have to think about work, or shopping, or what she will cook for dinner – she is on holiday. She chose this resort because the brochure claimed that it had (something for everyone) a balmy climate, a natural seascape, a beach unspoilt by commerce but with a modern hotel, with an infinity pool, a bar, a restaurant, even organised children's activities on two days of the week.

The sun is directly over the headland now, and Julie shades her eyes as she watches her youngest daughter running up the beach. Julie's last words to the children had been to follow the line of the last post on the promenade, and whatever they did, to 'stay together!' The latter command has been ignored, but at least Pippa is heading in the right direction. Julie signs off the postcard to her parents, refraining from saying that she wishes they were here.

It's so quiet now, apart from the rasping shriek of a gull. Here on the Vervain coast, the ocean enters the bay with a will of its own. Only the local fisherfolk can predict the point of the turning tide by the taste of the breeze, or the shade of the water, whether tinted by the churned sand or the glinting of the rainbow-scaled mackerel or, like today, darkened by the strip of a rip tide.

Julie shades her eyes and watches the progress of her youngest child running up the beach – she has still quite a way to go. Julie sighs and picks up her magazine and scans the contents. She picks out a story to read. She is attracted to the illustrations that run up the margins: swirly planets and symbols like Celtic knots. The story is based on real-life events that happened in the 1930s. It begins with a man who becomes lost in a forest. He meets others who have been living among the trees for so long that they have forgotten their old lives or even how much time has passed. There seems to be no way out, and so, with sadness, he settles down to life in the trees. One day, he finds a track that he has not noticed before, he follows it, and it leads him right out of the forest. His wife, rather than rejoicing at his return, is shocked by the state of his clothes and the length of his beard. He had only been gone for an hour. Julie looks at the before and after pictures: a man in his early thirties, clean-shaven, fresh-faced, with an arm around a woman, presumably his wife. And then, next to it, the face of a man probably in his late fifties, his features obscured by a grey beard, his hair unkempt. It could be the father of the younger man – the similarities in their eyes, the shape of the forehead.

Down at the tideline, the turret that lay squashed into the body of the castle needs to be repaired. Laura fills the bucket with sand, and tells Alfie to pat the top with his spade. She refills the bucket with damp sand, and together they make more castellations along the battlements. They have to work fast to remove the sand that is already filling the scoop of the moat. Laura remembers her sister, and looks up from her toil to assess the distance between Pippa and their mother. Pippa must have arrived back by now, as she is no longer in sight.

But Pippa is still running away from her sister and step-brother, and she does not want anyone to see that she is crying. But her tears are released with every judder of her feet on each crease and ridge of sand. Through her weeping, she hears the scream of the large gull overhead. Through her tears she can still make out the familiar shape of her mother, lying on her front propped up on her elbows. But every time Pippa looks, she seems to be further away. Pippa runs faster. She is gasping for breath. She must be at least half way there, but when she looks up again, it is as if there is a shimmering curtain between them. Everything has become muted, even her sobs and the beat of her heart are muffled. She can still see the gull. It is flying right above her; its mouth open as if it is screeching, but she can no longer hear it.

The gull hovers until it is drawn away by the thermals that have risen between the headlands.

Julie is engrossed with the story she is reading. The doctor sends the man from the forest for psychological tests.

There are other cases reported, and, before long, a team of scientists arrives at the village, and then other experts are brought in from various regions of the country. Before long, time sequencing equipment has been installed and is used to capture any changes in the forest's flora and fauna. Hours are made into seconds, days into milliseconds. Reels of films are produced and studied. Mediums and psychics and spirit channellers are consulted too. Could these people have been spirited away, kept in another time zone, and then restored to their previous lives? The study goes on for months, and those who have returned from the forest want answers – they still claim that they have lost years of their lives. Julie skips through to the end of the story. One conclusion is that the forest contains inexplicable pockets, lapses of time, the manifestation of portals.

The pages of the magazine ruffle, and Julie rolls it up and swats at a sandfly that is crawling along her shin. She pulls her sunglasses down from the top of her head. She senses a change in the breeze, and feels the burn of her shoulders against the cold edge of air. Julie stands up and reaches into the canvas bag for her cardigan. She looks towards the sea. She can barely make out the children now; they seem so far away. She screws up her eyes, increasing the contrast against the blur of sand and sea. Julie recognises the colours that the children wear: red trunks, a strip of blue, perhaps a costume, a yellow bucket – or is that a spade that is catching a glint? She can only see two of them, a boy and a girl of about the same height. But where is Pippa? She scans along the beach, one way and then the other, but she cannot see Pippa.

For Pippa, it seems a long time before the hard sand gives way to the softer sand above the high tideline and the ground underfoot seems a long way down. She feels awkward as if she has almost forgotten how to run, her head and shoulders are drawing her forward, but the rest of her body is lagging behind. The dry sand burns the soles of her feet as they push into the soft undulations; it is becoming harder and harder to move forward, her leg muscles extending to full stretch.

A gull lands on the sand near to Julie. 'Go away!' she shouts, but the gull continues to move towards her, and she picks up a stone and lobs it at the bird, missing it, and the gull remains. She throws another, again missing. This time the gull arches its wings and takes to the air, rising and disappearing in the haze. Julie follows the direction of the gull, then scanning the beach again, to the left, to the right, over by the rocks, even behind her in case the girl has come back without telling her and is playing on the dune. But no, there is no sign. Where's Pippa? Her stomach lurches; her heart is near to bursting as she gets up. She moves forward, at first stumbling, then walking, faster, and then running.

A girl, a tall, lean girl in her teens, is coming towards her.

'Have you seen..?' Julie cries out, but she can hardly speak she is so out of breath.

The girl throws her arms around her. She is crying, blubbering, incoherent.

'Let go of me,' Julie says. 'I'm sorry, but I need to find my daughter. Have you seen...?'

But she does not finish the sentence. The tall girl in front of her has the face of Pippa: it is tauter, but the expression, the eyes, the mouth, the jaw, are all Pippa.

Down at the sea's edge, Laura leans over the surf, dipping her bucket into the froth. Little by little it begins to fill, and beneath her the swell and the force of the draw-back increases. Her bucket is half full as its weight tips her forward. The pull of the waves undermines her, the muddied water reaches up and over her knees, sucking at her feet.

As she lifts up one foot, the other pushes in deeper, into the viscous seabed. Alfie watches Laura sinking into the sand, deeper with each ebb. He is standing on the mound of the castle that is now rounded by the waves. Soon the rippled sands part to make way for the ocean as the moat disappears beneath the swell.

Above them, the gull is swooping over the cliffs, diving and cruising along the bay, dipping in and out of the spiralling thermals. The tide has turned.

A Witness of Waxwings

She watches the flickering TV screen. A nature pro-
gramme about the journey of the waxwings. The
documentary maker shouts into the fluffy-capped mi-
crophone to overcome the noise of the helicopter. In her
mind's eye, she is there too, looking down at the swirling
of the ocean and the white water that defines the edges
of a tiny island amid miles and miles of sea. The camera
zooms in.

*These small birds are easily identified by their prominent
crests and yellow-tipped tails. We have followed them from the
far north, and now they have reached the island of Roae. It has
been uninhabited since the 1930s when the last of the population
was forced to leave or face starvation.*

The camera pans from left to right, encompassing the
island. A man looks up at them – for a moment she sees his
face, eyes squinting into the sun.

*The journey of the waxwings is one of a long and arduous
flight. But they have not come here to breed: they will feed on the*

rowan berries and the hips and haws before they go on their way.

A close-up shot.

See the yellow tip on the tail and the mask around the eyes.

She recognises the man. There are no trees here, just low bushes; there is nowhere to hide from the hovering eye of the camera, a bird of prey watching every movement.

The waxwings have landed to refuel.

She remembers the days of the heavy drinking, the hard love, the pain. The nights when he had been out with his friends and then afterwards – the whisky, and the conversations that became arguments, and whatever she said, whichever way she chose – to agree or disagree – it made no difference. The bruising was always below neck level, hidden under clothes, where only she knew. It was her fault because he told her it was. She might have prevented it if only she had stopped him. But the real bruises were far inside where they could not be revealed, where no one could see them. And then there was the next day – always apologies, the sorrow, the flowers, and her forgiveness, and then the making up – these were the rituals that had become their lives. But one day he went too far. He left, leaving his mark to yellow on her face. There was to be no apology, not this time, but then, she knew she could not forgive him, not ever.

She was left to the silence and the quiet creep of fear that he might return.

And now here he is, alone on a small rock, cowering, caught in the click of a shutter. He runs, climbing over a stile, tripping, picking himself up, stumbling along a track that follows the line of the cliff, and down a steep path towards a bay. Waves are lashing at the jetty, a boat flinching on the sea.

Soon the waxwings will be flying south in their search for food...

The helicopter is turning, side-on to the ocean, leaving the island, the boat, the man.

...and as they travel down the east coast of the mainland, they will raze the hedgerows and the gardens of their berries.

She will wait for the waxwings. They are her witness.

Sea Level

Far out in the Moray Firth, on the grey-blue sea, is a speck, a tiny black point. Abel can hear the buzz of an engine, like the drone of a bee; as it approaches the coast, it becomes a high-pitched snarl. A small motor boat leans, it turns and skims towards the landing jetty. Abel has got to know most of the seagoing crafts and their owners since his arrival over a year ago. But this one, heading into the crook of the bay, is unfamiliar; perhaps it is from further down the coast.

Some things are as potent as nature: brutal forces, born from ancient myth, surviving in rituals that go beyond living memory. And there are stories, those that are repeated from generation to generation, and there are rituals, like the blackenings before a wedding, and there are the rumours about mythical creatures, Selkies, emerging from the sea to claim the menfolk.

Abel thinks it would be ridiculous that anyone still believed in such tales. Folk have more to do than to be sitting around the fire telling stories these days; they have TV and the internet for their entertainment. In any case, if anyone thought they'd get Abel for a blackening, he would have heard about it. He feels sure that his friends, although he has made few, would not have been able to keep quiet. Even secrets find a way of seeping through the cracks in a place like this. But as the men crash onto the shingle, Abel is not so sure.

Five men: not locals, he would know them. He would recognise their shape, their movement. But these are not the lads from the salmon fisheries, nor are they the build-ers, nor the hotel staff from Bartown, nor even the sum-mer hangarounds. They wear black hoods, the kind that scubadivers wear. The sun reflects on their neoprene pelts as they leap out of the boat, swift and measured, onto the jetty. The smaller one ties the rope to a cleat on the edge of the seawall, and remains there as if standing guard. The others stride along the jetty, towards Abel, who stops what he is doing – knotting the twine to fix the creel – letting it fall from his hands.

One of the men carries a small tar barrel, another an old coal bag from which a few feathers escape; drifting, fluttering in the wind. The air is filled with the stink of fish guts. Abel feels the freeze in his blood – this time, of fear. The cottage is only a hundred yards away. He will run, bolt the door behind him, wait for them to disappear. His legs become heavy weights that hold him in one place. He scrambles on the shingle, a cartoon character, loose stones slipping with each forward motion, holding him back.

They say nothing, just surround him. 'Hey!' he shouts. 'You've got the wrong man!' but he is no match for the four men who are holding each of his limbs. He is stripped to his underpants, while they apply the contents of their bags and barrels, pouring and throwing them over him. His skin stings and cracks with the hardening of the sheep treacle. He is stuck with feathers: loose ones, escaping,

23

making him sneeze. Then there is the soot. He blinks through the black grit in his eyes. But worst of all is the fish guts, the rancid smell.

Still, the men have not spoken. One of them points to Abel's truck parked by the end cottage. They lift him up and carry him to the truck, throw him into the back. He always leaves the keys in the ignition: there's less chance of losing them. The men are intent, as if what they do is a duty, a job that must be done. The engine starts. It stalls, and for a moment Abel is relieved. But the truck has been left in first gear, so when it starts, it jolts forward and Abel rolls across the metal floor, stopped by the empty creels. Jolt. Second gear and they move forward, up the steep hill, bumping over the grit track. Abel thinks about trying to escape, but he can hardly move with the hardening tar on his body. Instead, he clings to the rope that is tied to the rung on the side.

But his mind is slipping, as if out of gear, just as she slipped out of his arms that time at the jetty. He watched her from above, flicking her legs, turning over and over in the sea, her long hair floating around her, tendrils of dark curls rising and wavering in the air.

He had been trying to start the motor on the skiff when he noticed a young woman was leaning over the end of the jetty. 'Are you OK?' he asked.

'Yes,' she replied but did not look up. 'I'm watching.'

She was trying to memorise the way each tiny ripple turned, how the waves lapped over the rocks beneath the surface, and how the bolder waves, the front runners, leapt up at intervals, spilling over the edge of the breakwater.

The girl leaned forward just as a large wave exploded up and over the jetty. Abel saw the wave as it spilt over her, and he knew that the drag of the retreat would pull her over the edge. He grabbed hold of her arms to save her from falling into the sea. He shivered as he pulled her closer to him. Her arms were slim and cold, unnaturally so, but his hands on her arms were burning, a burning that sears at the skin: the touch of ice. Another wave sent its spray up high, and there was a moment of stillness when he knew that something had changed in him forever. As he let her go, he felt uneasy, as if something had passed between him and this strange girl, as if their souls had met and he had entered into a bargain, that he had signed a contract that could never be withdrawn.

He is swung hard into the other side as the truck turns right. The four men in the cab are beeping the horn, calling and whistling. Abel can hear others joining in, shouting out and laughing, as they pass. Some of the voices he recognises: the lads from the salmon fisheries down by the harbour are shouting and jeering; the girls from May's restaurant are whooping. They turn, sharply reverse, turn again and roll on towards the stony beach past the last warehouse. They stop.

Abel had gone to The Mission House that day, a place that had been rented out for the summer. He was there to ask Mr Macpherson for the hand of his daughter in marriage. Macpherson said he was as surprised as anyone when his daughter announced that she had fallen in love. He had not expected her to want to stay for longer than the summer, let alone for the rest of her life. 'As soon as we arrived, Kelsie changed,' he declared. 'She ran onto the shingle bank. "I love the sea," she shouted, "I want to *be* the sea."'

'*Be* the sea?' Abel thought he'd heard wrong.

'That's what she said. Of course, it doesn't make sense,' Macpherson continued, 'but that's Kelsie for you.'

'She loves the sea; I do know that,' Abel said. 'That's what makes her special.'

'Hah!' But Macpherson thought otherwise. 'Well, I thought she'd soon find something more interesting than the ocean.' And as he said it, he slapped Abel on the back. 'And she did. She found you!' He laughed, overly loud as if he'd cracked a joke.

Abel is half tipped, half pulled out of the back of the truck. The men do not want to touch him, they push him along with their feet onto the bank of stones at the top of the beach, and then they return to the cab and drive away – their job done. Abel is bruised, battered in a sticky, stinky mess of guts and feathers and flour and soot, abandoned on a rocky beach in the curve of Gamrie Bay.

'There, there.' It's the voice of an old woman. 'The better the blackening, the longer the marriage,' she croons.

She is hunched over him, her face is hidden, white strands of hair escaping, wavering in the sea breezes. He hears little noises, like a whimpering, and he realises the sounds are coming from him.

'Up you get,' she says now. 'Get yourself into the water. Wash it all off, that's what the sea is for.'

He stumbles a little, but she helps him to the edge where he falls into a deep rock pool. He rubs his arms with sea water that is still warm from the last rays of the sun. He splashes it across his chest, rubs away at his skin, ducks his head beneath the surface, runs his fingers through his hair and over his face. Shaking away the droplets of water, at last, his skin is free. He looks over to the path that crosses the stony upper edge below the cliff, but the woman is nowhere to be seen. He wonders, for a moment, whether she has slipped behind him and into the sea, and even whether she is a Selkie. He shivers.

Abel, grandson of Abel the Fisher, stands where his ancestors stood, on rocks made smooth with the passage of water and time. The weather was forecast to be stormy, with high winds and a certainty of rain. No one ever assumes that nature will obey the meteorologists, not here, but the morning had indeed started with the wind and heavy rain, and black clouds rolled in to shore.

Abel is scrubbed clean and wears his best shirt and kilt, the tartan of the Black Watch. He shows no sign of his ordeal of the previous day, and he stands on the beach on the very spot where he stood yesterday, mending his creels. His beautiful bride is next to him. She wears a long cream dress; her hair is braided, her face glowing. She holds onto his arm, gently squeezing it, and he can feel the bruises he sustained from the blackening. He looks around at the crowd. There is only his family, his best man, his neighbours, and the clergyman standing before them, Bible in hand, waiting for the guests to gather around. The chattering continues until the roaring sea relents and the wind falters. Now, all is calm, the sun has warmed the beach, the waves purr, and the land and the sea are met in placid collusion.

'We are gathered here today,' the priest declares, holding up one hand, the other balancing the holy book.

All eyes are on the bride, the groom, the clergyman, the best man, the bride's father. Behind them, the sea lingers at the cusp of the turn, as if not daring to creep past the tideline of weed at the base of the pebble bank. For once, the sea is patient. The sun floats from behind a cloud, and the sea is transformed from tarnished silver to the grey-blue of the harebells on the cliff. Even as a backdrop, it has the grandest of parts: all sweetness against a winking light.

High tide. As the priest holds up his hand, the wind drops and all is calm. 'To all who are gathered, let us pray!' As the prayers come to an end and the 'amens' murmur along the bay, the wind recommences, and the sun catches the spray as it flicks up and over the jetty.

With the rings and kisses exchanged, the wedding party make its way to the Mission House. All the while the wind is riffling and batting, snatching at scarves, at hats.

But no one looks back at the sea, as the waters of the bay glint their green eyes. The guests are thinking only about the wedding feast, chattering, licking their lips in anticipation.

The long table is set: silverware glistens, white crockery is set off by a turquoise linen tablecloth. The centrepiece is a bouquet of dark blue irises studded with white gypsophila, and cream streamers spill over the place-settings like the manes of the white horses in the bay. Green silk ribbons flow down the sides of the table, and each plate and every glass are adorned with a cream ruff-edged napkin – the cresting of the waves.

The guests sigh when they see the room and how the table is decorated. They exclaim that it is a work of art, an ocean of beauty.

'It's all for you,' Kelsie's words linger on an icy breath in Abel's ear.

No one has noticed the old woman who has slipped into the room behind the others. But as soon as his eyes alight upon her, Abel recognises the face at once – she is the old woman on the beach. She is carrying a gift, a sealskin, sleek and fresh. The blood is iron fresh as if straight from the seal's back. A salty scent permeates the air. Abel opens his mouth, but he cannot speak. Kelsie, on the other hand, is smiling: 'It is the most beautiful, precious gift,' she says, taking it from the old woman, and stroking it against her cheek.

And out in the bay, the shadows flicker under the rolling waves, twisting and turning as if pulling at their deepest tetherings. The tide has turned. The waters of the bay are rising, coming closer, reaching the shore, seeping into the land, and rising some more.

Carapace

There were other departments in the museum, but she had no interest in the sepia photos taken at the time of the Gold Rush: the men with their pickaxes, staring beyond the camera, the women in long gowns, sleeves rolled up revealing muscular arms, panning arms, ones that sifted through the tons of stone brought to the surface. That was history. Below ground, there was pre-history – the history that belonged to the land, the dirt, the soil, the desert. It was more of a catacomb, an ossuary, a grand collection of bones, sorted into categories according to species and tagged accordingly.

Ava was on the lower ground level where the musty smell reminded her of all the underground places she been to before: caves, tunnels, grottos, potholes. Something drew her here, an uncanny magnetism that brought her back, time and time again. She never went on holiday anywhere else. It was always to this desert town where the only other tourists were the ones who were dispatched from their buses for a comfort stop of fifteen minutes, no more. The one-stop café had no air-conditioning, and the counter had a scattering of dead flies. The service was slow, so slow that many gave up, and left, hungry and thirsty.

The museum opened early on weekdays, and closed for long siestas that stretched beyond the hourly clatter of the chapel bell. Ava was there, just as the museum opened. The conservator came to greet her. He had been expecting her. He'd already opened the door to the vault. She walked down the stone steps, sighing as if she had come home. Straightaway, she looked for the piece that she'd come all this way to see. The carapace, the hood of bones that once contained the body of the ancient creature, the giant of the genus, which had lived for two hundred and fifty years and was the last of the species.

Her friends could never understand her fascination with the remains of an extinct giant, nor why she kept returning every year as if to pay homage. If only they would visit, they would understand the things that mattered; the beauty and grace of a race that had existed long before them. At this very moment, they would be working in their offices, typing up minutes, filing papers, speaking to customers on the phone, measuring their days in weeks and tea-breaks, ticking them off as if living a race that stretched from one year end to the next. And their holidays, booked for a fortnight in the summer, to places that catered for their comfort and entertainment. Wouldn't she be better to go on a cruise, a holiday for singles, where she'd meet people, people who were alive? What was so special about old bones? They asked her, curious, perplexed, but no time to listen. And why would she want to visit a pile of calcified matter: skulls, femurs, ball joints, ribs? Even she did not know the answer.

Ava looked for the alcove where the carapace was kept. Her blood slowed as she saw it. It was just like the first time: its beautiful frilled edge like an embellishment, an ancient bonnet, a hood that had sheltered the oldest of creatures. From here, the scaly neck would stretch out from under its sheltering hull, slowly turning from side to side, viewing the world in its measured stride, taking in every insect, bird, bush, every grain of sand, and then returning – to the carapace.

Clock, Time, Stop

The bodily presence of the departed is gone forever, but their essence lingers in the objects they touched during their lifetime.

Raya read the quote. It was typed on a piece of paper and stuck onto the back of the bottle. The brown glass had clouded, and the label on the front had long since peeled away. She pulled out all the other contents of the box. The dust of a score of years billowed into her face, and she breathed the musty air entombed for all that time. She stared at the clock. The hands were still. They had probably stopped soon after Jack's heart burst, or when her own heart raged with grief and anger, and time became a black hole.

Jack had discovered the art of French-polishing from a man at a street market in Nijmegen. He had come home enthused, albeit with an almost empty van. Raya was mad at him.

'You paid how much?'

'You should have seen it,' Jack said. 'You'd have felt the same.'

Raya was not sure. Jack with his romantic notions; spellbound by a cabinet glimmering in the sunlight like stilled water.

'So much for picking up furniture for a song,' Raya said.

It was hardly worth the expense of the ferry fare and the diesel. As well as the art nouveau mantel clock, there was a shiny cabinet that looked as if it would be more at home in a château – too ornate for their customers. The plan had been for Jack to buy cheap furniture from markets and auctions, and together they would do it up and sell it on, making a neat profit. They already had the beginnings of a lucrative business, and their shop window displayed some choice pieces: a breakfast table with barley-twist legs, a solid mahogany side table, a Victorian bedstead, and two Welsh dressers. The latter were sought by young professionals.

To begin with, Jack collected everything he would need: jars of flaked shellac, bottles of ethanol, linseed oil, brushes, sanding pads, wadding. He began with the clock; it was German made, with a fine rosewood case, also from the market in Nijmegen. Its plain sides were ideal for practising his French-polishing skills, and the dark rosewood responded by producing a fine lustre. The mechanism was rusty, but if he replaced the cogs, it would tick and chime once again.

Perhaps it was a coincidence, but it wasn't long after acquiring the clock that Jack began to act rather strangely. It was nothing that Raya could quite put her finger on, just a general restlessness. Night after night, Jack rubbed the polish into the wood, silently, working with the grain, careful not to spoil the veneered-edge pattern around the clock face.

All that was a long time ago. After the accident, Raya had packed away Jack's belongings and sent them to a charity shop – apart from the clock and a few other bits and pieces. She had put those in a box, and stowed it away in the attic to be forgotten. Raya had apparently gotten over the shock of losing Jack – too quickly, according to her friends – moving on, never mentioning him in conversation. Now, when she opened the lid, it was as if those memories that had been stuffed inside were released, rising into the air, filling the space, and, as with Pandora's box, she knew that once those memories were released, she could no longer put them back. If she had been asked an hour ago what might be in the box, she would have said: 'It'll be just a few old tins of boot polish, brushes, string, old laces – all that kind of stuff – things waiting to be fixed – rubbish really.'

But she would not have mentioned the clock, or indeed, the letters. They had arrived for Jack afterwards, and in her upset she had stowed them away, pushing them out of her mind.

The odours of polish, spirits and wax seeped into the air, spreading like spores. As she breathed in, she felt them filling the deep recesses of her mind. She jumped at a sound. A click. There it was again, this time more of a tick, and slowly, the ticks gathered, picking up speed. Tick, tick, tick, faster and faster – as if moments of time were fast-forwarding, catching up, striving to reach into the future.

Raya began to see things, moments, glimpses of the past: like the time when she and Jack went to visit her aunt at Westcliff-on-Sea, and how Jack's interest was drawn to the sundial in the garden. In her mind, she could see his hand, the familiar pattern of veins under the tanned skin, and the way his fingers lingered on the gnomon as it cast its shadow on the dial plate. She remembered the smell of his sweat as together they moved across the living room floor on their knees hand-sanding the old oak boards – despite his mother's derision and insistence that it would be too draughty in winter and that a good wool carpet would be far more sensible. Such moments she had not thought about for a long time, and it surprised her. It was as if all her senses were expelling their memories at once, leaving her spinning. She thought she might be sick. Now, having arrived in the present, the clock's ticks became regular, having made up for the lost time. Raya stood up, she stumbled forward – she had to escape, to get out of the attic, but the heat overcame her.

She must have fainted. Odd, she thought, because that had never happened before. She wasn't the fainting sort. She came round with her face pressed against an old doormat, and when she put her hand to her cheek, it felt stippled. She looked around the attic room; there were pictures stacked up against the walls, a stepladder lay at a tilt against the chimney breast, an old washboard, and dusty enamel plates in a pile on the floor; everything just as it was. She rubbed her face and pressed the palms of her hands against her eyes. She was left with the flotsam: a residue of images, sounds, tastes. 'Jack,' she whispered, not knowing why, but all she heard was the echo of her voice, hoarse and trill through the motes of dust.

She pushed the clock and the letters and all the other bits and pieces back into the box, stuffing an old pair of pyjama bottoms around the clock to protect it, and then she began to carry the box down the stairs. She thought about cleaning the clock, how she would need to warm the wood, soften the varnish, wipe it with spirits. Then she would polish it with shellac, not the aerosol she used for the dining table; that would only dissolve the lustre. No, she would do it the way that Jack had. 'Put love into all you do, and love will find its way back twofold,' he had said. Certainly the case for Jack, she thought wryly.

Back then, the furniture restoration business had been popular. As fashions are prone – even in the furniture world – it had come full circle: the desire for modern fitted furniture was declining, and in its place was an appetite for the stand-alone pieces of previous decades. Jack and Raya needed to find new supplies, and that meant going abroad: to French markets, Belgian auction houses, Dutch flea markets, house clearances. Jack went over to the Continent once a month, and Raya stayed behind to look after the shop. He always phoned on arrival, and again as he was leaving. Sometimes it was necessary to extend his visit to catch a sale in a nearby town. Raya always believed him.

'Only a hop across the Channel,' Jack said the first time. 'I'll be back before you know it,' he said with a wink.

On that final trip, Raya had driven him to the ferry port. Jack was going to hire a van on the other side this time. There had not even been a chance to say goodbye. A quick peck on the cheek as she checked her wing mirror, and then Jack disappeared through the swing doors of the ferry terminal.

Now she was sitting on the top stair with the open box on her lap, one hand resting on the clock. Its cold surface warmed to her touch, cool but soft, like skin. She had watched Jack polishing the casement, his arm muscles lightly flexing, his hands working over the wood. She touched her arms, her shoulders, the top of her breasts. She sighed. It had been so long. After they made love, his scent would remain on her skin, sometimes all day. His essence remaining with her, in her.

The stair carpet had become worn over the treads, and in some places only the stringy weft fibres were left. But when she slipped Raya did not let go of the box. It tipped forward, spilling old theatre tickets, birthday cards, a penknife, a spectacles chain. All went clattering and shimmying down the stairs. The last thing to escape was a photo: black and white. Like a magpie escaping a hijacked nest, the photograph glided at first, before fluttering and landing on the patterned tiles below. She looked through the balustrade. The photograph had landed face-up. Jack was looking up at her from below. He was on the deck of a ship, smiling, with a teasing glint of sun on his teeth. The sky above him was white; it must have been a clear day. His arms held out, his hands open, beckoning her towards him. For a moment she could feel the warmth of his breast as they hugged; she could hear the beat of his heart. He was wearing the shirt she had bought him for his birthday, the one with the thin blue stripes, their lines made up of tiny printed birds. He had said he would only wear it on special occasions.

Raya thought she heard someone laughing, a rhythmical sound in tune with the water lap-lapping at the edge of the hull, but soon it became muffled by the drone of the turbines. The ship had entered the deep-water channel before anyone had noticed the water trickling through the unsealed bow door. The gulls were soaring overhead, their high-pitched screams ululating, and, for a moment, she believed she was on the deck, walking towards him – but then the rumble of the engines became the rocking of the kettle boiling on the stove, the screaming gulls the steam hissing through the whistle.

Jack was long gone, and since then she had stripped the house of everything that reminded her of him. But here he was in this clock. Her fingers lingered over the veneered patterning and around the edge of the face. She shivered. The heating had broken down last winter, and she had not bothered to get it fixed. She placed the box, with the clock inside it, in front of the fireplace in the living room and began to gather everything she could find to make a fire: newspaper, her collection of wooden lovespoons, the broken clothes horse. Finally, she pulled the loose panel off the back door and placed it on the top of the pile. She struck a match, but, at first, the heap merely smouldered. Then she remembered that she'd heard somewhere that sugar could be used to start a fire, so she tipped out the last granules from a packet. She had to keep pushing everything back, so nothing would fall out, but gradually the fire began to spit, and the draught from the hole in the back door fanned the flames.

Finally, she sat by the hearth, the clock in her lap, rubbing it gently with the cloth. She added a few drops of linseed oil and began to rub. That would be all that it would take to release Jack's breath, the sweat of his hands, a stray eyelash, all his essences embalmed in shellac. As the clock warmed with the heat from the fire and the motion of her hands, its tick found a regular rhythm. By the time the fire had begun to die down, the surface of the clock was warm. She leant forward, placed her cheek against it, and it felt soft and warm, it smelt of flesh, and it trickled – with sweat.

Raya looked at the photograph next to her on the floor. Its glossy surface had rippled, and a spit from the fire had burned a hole where Jack's face had been. He was still beckoning to the photographer, but he was no longer Jack; just a faceless person calling to a person behind a camera, and now, when the shutter was pressed, he would be gone. The ticking of the clock slowed, and when it finally stopped, she let it slip from her hands.

Beast Market

The traders rock from side to side in their skin boots: their limbs padded, their bodies swathed in wadding. They stand hunched, in bunches along the back of the stalls, swinging their arms and slapping them across their bodies; hugging in the warmth, stamping their feet on the ground. Today's temperature is the lowest of the winter so far.

I lay out the bric-a-brac: ornaments, lampshades, leather purses, items embossed with the names of places I have never visited – and nor am I likely to – the monikers of foreign places. At the front of the stall are the smaller items, the ones I love: shiny brass bangles, necklaces, beads, trinkets – the keepsakes of a kind that no one keeps for long. Things that have been collected, begged, swapped, and occasionally stolen from the nests of others.

The air has a menacing, bitter edge. Even so, the sun shines through, too brightly – a searing white neither like heat nor freeze – some twist in the climate. The snows have retreated quickly, almost overnight, and the town is covered in a glaze, peaked in the corners, dripping from railings, forming a sheering of ice.

'Stay here and do not leave the stall.' Father's last instruction.

I am left under the watchful eye of Shiri while Father tends his 'important' business.

'Keep an eye on my flighty daughter,' he says.

For him, there are always people to meet: deals to make and sometimes break. He says I bring him luck, and he taps the side of his nose as if we share a secret. As we drew into town in the first shadows of dawn, Father slowed as we neared the horses. Some were tied to posts; others corralled within wicker fences. Small boys were brushing down the horses' coats, slicking over any imperfections; the older ones were chiding and cursing their beasts to make them walk in a perfect circle, heads up. I guess Father will be there now – at the Beast Market. It is always the same. Father never brings home a horse or even a cow or a sow or a gaggle of geese – but, somehow, a deal has been done. Some poor creatures have been bought and sold or exchanged and sold on again. He is a master of his trade. Today he has brought a cage.

The town in the valley had once been famous. Where the market now stands was a grand palace built by the King of Trin. It had tiered roofs, gardens, waterfalls, fountains and pools of rainbow fish. There were steam rooms and saunas and deep pools of icy water for visitors to steep their bodies, rejuvenate their flesh. The king invited many and welcomed those who wished to hunt in the forests for the deer and the wild hogs. The sides of the slaughtered animals were hung in the shady hallways to dry, or were salted, or smoked in the charcoal burners. The king's chefs created pies and puddings that are still famous throughout the region.

As small children, we gathered in the Great Hut to sit at the feet of Molam, the storyteller. Every year in the springtime, he left his cave in the upper valley and strode down to the towns and villages to tell his stories for a few coins or a meal. He delighted us with his tales of the lands beyond the mountains, where the great rivers divided and filled the soil with sweet minerals. He told us how our country had once been abundant with flora and fauna: exotic creatures, birds of many colours, plants and flowers that contained all the shades of oil on water. And he told us about the precious emerald gems set along the pathways of the valleys and how they reflected the numerous shades of green of the viridescent glades. And he told us about the special bird whose wings sparkled and glinted as it flew across the verdant land.

In Molam's stories, every bird belonged to the king and it was forbidden to kill any of them. Cages stretched along the whole side of the palace, and it was here that the most exotic birds were kept and bred. One day, the king received a gift of a pair of rare emerald flute-birds. A special cage was made for them, and the king hoped that they would breed. But no matter how much their surroundings emulated the forest, how luxurious were their furnishings, how soft was the velvet of their mossy perches, or how abundant the array of freshly cut branches, the truth was that they were unable to breed whilst held captive. Eventually, the male bird died and the female simply disappeared. But over the centuries many people have claimed to have seen the ghost of the female flute-bird as she returns to the wooded valley each evening after searching for her lover, her green wingtips flashing like jewels in the evening light.

By mid-morning, I am almost unable to move from my stool. I am hunched inside the collar of my hair coat, my neck retracted. The cold has worked its way into my bones; the pump of my tiny heart is barely able to shift the stream of icy blood. The drip on the end of my nose has all but frozen into a sharp point.

Now I am so cold; I believe I will be paralysed – fixed to my stool forever. Balanced on my haunches, I hug my knees. The stool rocks and almost tips. No one has bought anything from the stall today, but that is not surprising – none has the leisure to linger over trinkets: paste jewels, necklets of copper, the boxes of unworn or once-worn rings now dulled in this bitter air. The market cats arrive in a clowder. I have a terrible fear of cats. I pull the great coat around me as they sniff along the edges of the stalls and slip around the hallway like a team of wily thieves.

Shiri is on the next stall. She has not seen the cats. She knows how I feel about them and often she will let me hide in her barrow of rugs. Now she has a customer, and she is running her hand along a bolt of cloth, showing the neatness of its weave. The customer is frowning at the price, pursing her lips, offering too little. Poor Shiri! She tries so hard to make a living. Each week she brings the items her family have collected and re-made from rags – cut up, patched or embroidered to cover a stain. She likes to catch the eye of a passer-by, calling to them, suggesting they might like this lovely throw or that patchwork bedcover, or a pictorial wallhanging to decorate their home.

'Go for a walk, Birdy,' Shiri suggests. 'You need to move about or you'll catch cold.'

She hands me a cup of hot maize from her flask. She looks into my face below the peak of my hood.

'It's fine,' she says. 'I will watch the stall.'

'I'll be back as quick as I can,' I say. 'You won't...'

'No, I won't say anything.' She knows I mean Father. 'Don't worry,' she says. 'Go, little Bird, go.'

She always calls me Birdy because I am so small and slight. My feet are tiny like an infant's, never having grown out of their first pair of shoes. And once, when she brought dates and seeds for a snack, I ate the whole lot. She was not cross; she merely declared that I must have needed them more than she did because I have no fat on me. Once, when she had cause to lift me up, she declared: 'You're as light as a tiny bird!'

I wander away as Shiri plays a tune on her ocarina; the tiny notes gather in the vessel and stream through the myriad of pathways that form the maze of Poco Market. The stalls around the edges are open to the sky and, like mine, they sell goods that were once owned by others. A cornucopia of overflowing tables surrounds the established vendors – those who have a covering of canvas. Some are enclosed within large marquees where customers browse through the goods, whiling away their time as they shelter from the vagaries of the weather. There are stalls that sell fresh meat, eggs, cheese, pastries, cakes, painted tableware, glassware: everything a new couple could need to set up their household. The centre of the market has a roof, of sorts, held up by a framework that once shouldered the great carved beams that made the market famous throughout the region.

I am almost through to the other side of the market when I begin to feel the warmth. The heat is coming from a brazier whose flames are reflected in daubs of orange and yellow on the flagstones. A group of men is gathered around it; they are smoking, spitting onto the ground. Some are shaking hands; some are leaving. Several youngsters are seated on a raised plinth below a bar to which the horses are tied. They swing their legs and pass a bottle from one to the other. On one side are goats housed in pens; they nudge at the pens with their horns. The smoke that comes from the fire is bitter, almost acrid, but even so, I enjoy the sharp tang as it hits my senses. I am near enough to the stalls at the edge not be noticed. This is the Beast Market.

A man picks up a plank of tarred wood and throws it

into the fire. There is a crack and a spit of tar that shoots out across the yard. It lands at my feet. I shriek. The men fall silent for a moment. They resume their conversation. Then others join them, talking in an unfamiliar dialect. But there is one voice I know well among the quick, guttural sounds – my father's voice. He has not seen me, and I duck below a stall and peer over the tabletop. The conversation continues, each time petering out until it is snatched up by the others as if it must be grabbed and tackled to the ground. These men must be from over the Purling Mountains judging by their gowns of heavy grey and brown stripes. I have heard that up in the mountains they speak few words for fear of catching a cold. Perhaps, the valley air does not compare with the freezing temperatures to which they have become familiar. Their voices are raised as if they are jostling to own the words, but still, I have no idea what they are saying.

Father is at the centre of the crowd, and he is arguing with a tall man. I try to slip by, but they are filling the whole space of the aisle between the stalls. They are gesticulating, and their voices are raised. Then others begin to push, butting each other in the chest with open hands. It seems that something has been stolen, and the tall man is demanding its return, but Father is waving some money in his face and shouting as if it is he who has been hard done by.

A bird, the colour of emeralds, appears from between them as if conjured from the heat of the fray. The men turn towards it, and for a moment all is quiet again as they stare at the bird who has landed on a stall of corn dollies and miniature scarecrows. The bird pecks at the straw – once, twice – before a strand is released from the tightly woven manikin.

The bird calls in a single clear note and flutters in front of me. Its fan of soft tails brushes across my face. The feathers tickle, and I laugh. A tingling sensation has spread around my body as if it is coming from the inside. My blood is no longer stiff, my limbs are free and light, and I feel my heart quickening.

The stall-holders and their customers are looking up as I ascend into the roof. But the men are rushing around, their arms wide open, pushing each other, running in circles and from side to side. They are all trying to capture the bird. They are looking everywhere: under the stalls, behind the barrels, into the rafters. There is only one who has not moved and who continues to stare in my direction. It is Father. He is holding a bundle of notes in one hand and in the other hand, a cage. I look down at him from my perch on the purlin. His eyes are dark gems, gleaming. I am afraid to be so high above the ground, and I call out.

'Father! Father! Catch me.'

He stares up. He does not take his eyes from me for a moment as he opens the door of the cage. Around my neck is a thick bristling ruff, but it moves easily, each feather gliding against the other. I look at my arms and see that they are cloaked in the fine green feathers of a fledgling, and I wonder if my wings are strong enough to take me back to Shiri.

Father has not seen her. Shiri is standing a little way behind. Her hands are clasped around the ocarina; the notes flutter in the air. The tune is one I have never heard before. It rises, then floats, then lifts up as if in a proclamation: fly free, Birdy, fly free. The song of the ocarina curls around the rafters, over the heads of the market traders, out through the market, across the town, as I follow the course of the swift river towards the shiny jewels of the viridescent forest.

Mother Tongue

The house is just how she remembers, smaller, perhaps. Inhaling deeply, she pauses for a second and listens to the rhythm of the cicadas in the long grass. For years, her only music has been the whistle of the icy air ululating over snow-smothered flatlands.

It wasn't her wish. Decisions like that cannot be made by a child.

'We can no longer stay here,' he'd said. 'We leave tomorrow.'

She ran to the barn, sought the darkest corner, hid until found.

Of the journey, she knows of the leaving.

Memories: her mother is saying, 'not for long, it won't be for long,' and hugging her tightly, too tightly. Her own hand raised as if in surprise as she is waving to all that is familiar, saying goodbye to everything she has known: the little room where she sleeps that looks onto the yard, the kitchen with the cracked tiles where every morning she has eaten bread fresh from the oven, the doorstep where she likes to sit and bounce a ball against the far wall.

She waves to the dog running along the track beside them as they drive away in her father's car, their belongings strapped to the roof, crammed inside with just enough space for her in the back. And she waves to the old man pushing the bicycle and staring at them with his sad, milky eyes, and the tree with the swing, and even the chickens. All that she is left with is the fragrance of the soil at the end of the day, lingering in her mouth, her nose, her mind.

After that, there was the dark hull on a black sea, waking to the sound of the ship's horn echoing in an unknown harbour, the grandmother she'd never met, the place of juddering syllables, guttural utterances, petering sounds, a land of shadows. A language she would never learn to speak – the language of snow, of ice, of clipped vowels. No wonder she felt silenced, muted, hushed by shadows of isolation. She could no longer speak.

And now the time has passed, she has returned to the sandy hills of her childhood, and she will regain her tongue's memory; she yawns in the soft familiar air, her speech returns.

Sprite

It was Cousin Jem who found the body floating down the river. He came back hollering, and we all rushed to see what the to-do was about. The older boys waded out, and the rest of us stood there gawping, and for once nobody spoke, but I could feel their eyes shifting.

Even as the body was lugged to the sandy edge, I hoped it was an animal. It was not unknown for one to escape from a field where the old walls give way, their top stones shifting, leaving the weather to erode the rest. One time a sheep got into the next field, surprised as the bracken gave way underfoot and it tumbled and rolled down the sides so steep that nothing could stop its final plunge into the gorge.

But this was no sheep.

I heard the birdsong, the water pooling in the shallows around each waxy stem. Then everything stopped. I was looking at a swollen torso; naked, skin bloated and white.

It could have been a manikin, stolen from a shop of

horrors: a white-faced ghoul, a zombie. It was as white as the alabaster statue of the grotto at the crossroads.

'Better fetch the copper,' Jem said, breaking our silence. He was staring into the water as if staring would make it go away.

'The lad's dead,' Father said.

'Who is he?' a child asked.

Like the shed skin of a snake, this was a mere shell of a body. From its mouth spouted river weed as if the boy had choked, and his hair rippled over the stones in the shallows as if it was alive. The eyes were wide open and blue. I shivered. I looked down. Too late. I saw my reflection captured in their orbits.

It was here, this exact place, this little bay in the river, where my life had begun – or so I was told. According to tradition, the first born girl is a gift from the river. Why that should be I have no idea, but I believed it, utterly, until I was about ten years of age.

As a small child I had imagined myself as spawn on the river bed, nudged and scooped into a soft mouth of a fish and brought to the surface, cushioned inside a bubble and rolled along inside a transparent sphere, legs crossed, hands pressed against the slippery edge. I would be watching as the surface of the water came in and out of focus, seeing the world for the first time through a convex lens, ducking down as the dragonflies and damselflies flittered by, my reflection in the baubles of their eyes. There were water-boatmen with skittering legs, avoiding me as they danced the skin of the stillest pools, disappearing with a nudge of the breeze. I imagined my cries lulled by the fall of rain, droplets of water entering my squally mouth. But really, how could any of this be true? I understand the significance of a river, but not how a person could come from a river; be conceived, birthed by it.

Perhaps my birth happened as the bubble snagged on

a protruding root, or was buffeted into a whirlpool, spinning faster and faster until my temporary home had burst. One prickly branch, one protruding piece of grit would be all that it would take, and then I'd be plunged under the water but rise abruptly to the surface, head first, mouth blinking open, only to slip back again into this baptismal pool.

However it happened, my first cry was heard on a dry river bank where I was at the mercy of the wilderness, not only the vagaries of weather but the wildlife: stoats, voles, foxes, even the snatching pike. A woman (the one I now call Mother) was collecting reeds to weave into baskets to sell at the market. She gathered me up and wrapped me in her shawl and took me home. There I met my new family who greeted me with prods and pinches.

But the story changes with each telling, and now I believe that they never intended to keep me, at least, not forever. After all, no one wants an extra mouth to feed. I was to serve as the mascot, the lucky charm for our company of travellers; the one brought out on special days.

When pressed, my mother said that I was conceived 'because' of the river. Then, I'd imagine my parents slipping away from the others, holding hands, running along the river bank until they were out of sight. There would be a blanket on the ground, an opened bottle of stout, or whatever they'd smuggled away, and then the kisses and more kisses.

There are clues. I carry the river's name: Zabrina. Someone once told me that it is the Latin word for Severn and that it goes back to beyond the Iron Age (when Sabrina was the goddess of the river when, in ancient times, her rolling waves were mounted by a great sea horse deity). My name was another difference I bore with shame. All my siblings had names that came from the Bible.

Nevertheless, there is something about this story, an essence of veracity. The water of this river has a presence like no other; not merely a ditch or a narrow valley, but a gathering place for a liquid force ample enough to maintain life. I believe that the blood that courses through my veins brings with it the imprint of the river's spirit. Like my first memory; it runs through my dreams, and at night I am carried on its wave, rocked on the surface.

Every year, on this day, we go to the river; my mother, my father, my aunts and uncles, my cousins, my brothers and sisters. My first arrival on the river bank coincided with the balmiest month when the fields glowed with the pastel hints of cornflowers and campions, and there were foxgloves and the hedgerows gleamed with buds, all assured that the sleety blasts of winter were gone until the following year.

We carried vast amounts of food and blankets in wheeled barrows from the roadside to the pathway that led to the river bank. We set up camp as if we planned to stay a while, but we would only be there for a day. A shelter in the form of a bender was built from the overhanging branches; a tarpaulin was thrown across two bendy saplings and pinned to the ground with wooden pegs. Here, we would have shelter or shade where we would eat, drink, sing our songs. With our skirts tucked up and the youngsters stripped off without a care, we'd play in the shallows, giggling at the minnows darting between our toes. If one of us were to slip on a stone, we would grab another's sleeve, and soon all would have fallen into the ice-cold water, gasping and laughing and then we'd be up and chasing each other along the bank. Other times, we would stopper the water by building a dam and a pool that was deep enough to swim in.

This is how I remember my birthdays. I am no longer concerned with the old story of how I arrived on the river bank, like a water baby, a sprite. This is a day to be celebrated – but there is something odd – it is my thirteenth, but no one has mentioned it. My maturity is stunted, it seems I am to remain a child forever. I have barely grown an inch since my infancy.

I sit alone on the bank and watch the others leaping and shrieking and dunking one another in the water as I tip elderberry juice into my mouth. Everything stops. I swallow, but it is already too late. A cloud has drifted over with a darkening shadow.

"There'll be trouble to pay for this," I hear my aunt say.

She is already pulling the young ones away from the bank, and the smaller children are turning and yanking at her arms wanting to see. I stand by and watch the men lift the body up and onto the bank. My father takes off his jacket and lays it over the body, covering the face, the torn pocket playing in the wind. Then the men turn and wander back towards the big bender.

I am alone by the river, this giver of life, my life. And now, it had taken its due. But it is as if it does not know, that nothing has happened judging by the way it tinkles over the stones, carelessly frothy and giggly. I kick and stamp my feet at the water's edge.

After a while, I too walk back to the camp, but I keep looking back over my shoulder to see if the body remains. The river darkens and rushes a little faster each time I turn.

Everyone is quiet back at the camp; even the babies are mute. The men have gathered in the bender, and I creep around the back, but I can hear no voices. All is silent apart from the rain as it spits on the fire stones. Then someone speaks. My father's voice. 'Where's Zabrina? This will be to do with her.'

I feel a tightening in the pit of my stomach as I hunker in the brambles and listen to the voices.

'She's luck; she's our sprite, Zabrina is our river sprite.'

'Luck only lasts until it runs out.'

'The river will take again unless she is returned.'

'The river reclaims. We all knew that, someday...'
'Zac, go and fetch Zabrina!' my father commands.

I leave my sandals on the edge of the river bank and I step into the ice-cold water. I place my feet onto the larger stones to gain my balance but one of them rocks and I slip, twisting my ankle, but it does not hurt for long – the icy water cools the swelling. I am soon near the other side where the water is darkest and deepest, and I know what I must do.

My shoulders sink, and their blades clench. It is deeper than I thought. I am descending, and when I look up, I can no longer see the surface through the flickering green. An eel passes, curling by, and I see the bottom where the crayfish live. I watch their spawn from my sandy seat, and I hold out my hand to them.

I have been here for a long while, and I have not thought to take a single breath.

Creels

Evie wiped away the condensation that had formed on the cabin window with her sleeve. Now she saw the island. It was framed in the round pane of glass, and she could just make out the mountains, surrounded by rocky protrusions that rose from the sea. Clouds like curling smoke circled the peaks. She pulled Bunny closer to her and peered out through the ears. As the ferry drew closer, she saw a row of tall buildings that leaned into a curve around the harbour, stark against the slaty hills.

From the harbour wall, people were casting their fishing lines. Their waders glistened in the sun; their buckets of bait balanced on the edge of the quay. Others were hoicking round caskets from the hulls of the fishing boats, passing each, one to another, hauling them up over the edge. The two men who waited at the top stacked them along the quayside. They worked to a rhythm, and Evie could hear them calling to one other, almost musically; notes which cut through the drone of the engine.

The ferry edged towards the slope of the landing jetty and slowly lowered its bow door. There was a great creaking and clanging of metal as it grated against the jetty. The noise caused a commotion among the community of seabirds. Their wings batted against the vessel as a mechanical voice sputtered from the speakers:

'We are now docking at the Port of Barreth. Will passengers please disembark, taking all items of luggage with them?'

As Evie pulled her small trolley case up the gangplank and along the cobbled quay, its wheels kept catching between the raised stones, tipping and turning.

'Evie! Watch out!' Ma said. Evie tried to follow the smoothest path through, avoiding the coiled ropes that lay like snakes and the winches with metal bolts that protruded from the ground. 'Look where you're going!' Ma urged. But Evie was as careful as she could be, and when she looked up, she noticed that her mother was looking all around, glancing up and then down the pier, flinching at the scream of a gull.

There were many barrels stacked along the harbour wall, as well as the detritus of the fisherfolk. On the quayside were several crates, open-weave baskets that dripped with seaweed. Evie paused and peered through the dark slits of the creels. She jumped back as a claw shot out, and she watched the pincer open and snap shut. She shrieked and then giggled, and moved quickly on to catch up with her mother who was by now much further ahead.

'What are they?' Evie asked her mother when she had caught up.

'Lobsters,' Ma replied.

'Why are they in cages? Will they be allowed to go back to the sea?' Ma ignored her, and they continued to drag their wheeled cases along the quay, but Evie kept looking back at the pots with the waving tentacles.

The Harbour Hotel was straight ahead of them, and

soon they were through the doors. The smell of fish and the sound of gulls were exchanged for a buttery odour and the insipid tones of piped music. They approached the desk. By now Ma was panting, and her face was pink. She slapped the heel of her hand onto the bell, and it pinged in response, then deadened with the slump of her hand.

A woman appeared from beneath the counter. She was about the same height as Evie, so Evie reckoned, and she wondered if she had been playing hide-and-seek.

'And who do we have here?' the little woman said with a friendly but quizzical lilt to her voice.

Ma perked up, the tension releasing from her face as she spelt out her name. The woman smiled and pulled herself up onto a stool. Now Evie had a good view of her, but she winced when she noticed how tightly the dark hair was scraped back around the woman's ears – so tight that it made tiny bumps in her skin. The receptionist opened the book that was on the desk; it was wider than the span of her arms, and she needed both hands to fold over the page. She took a pencil, and with a flick of her wrist she had ticked the page.

'There we are,' she said. 'All nicely booked in. I'll show you to your room.' She looked down at the two small suitcases. 'You'll be able to manage them?' Ma said yes, they would.

The woman's eyes, which were like chocolate buttons, Evie thought, flitted towards the toy rabbit. The head had flopped over Evie's arm as if the neck was broken.

'What's his name?' she asked

'Bunny,' Evie said. 'She's called Bunny.'

Evie remembered her rag doll, Angel, as she watched the seamed lines on the back of the stockinged legs as they ascended the staircase. Evie remembered that she had left Angel on the bed in her bedroom, and her lips quivered when she thought of her, and how far they had travelled since leaving home.

The hotel room was all shades of pink in the early evening light. Through the window the last of the sun could be seen hovering on the horizon; streamers of orange and grey streaked the sky. Evie placed her elbows on the window ledge and pressed her face to the glass. She looked down at the harbour. Across the road were rows of empty cages stacked two abreast, piled six or so high. While the hotel lady talked to her mother about the room and told her the times for breakfast, Evie pushed the window from its latch, letting in the salty scents and the sounds of the harbour.

When she turned around, the receptionist had gone, and Ma was on her knees looking under the beds.

'What are you looking for?' Evie asked.

'Nothing,' Ma replied, bobbing up and speaking in a soft voice, almost a whisper.

Evie turned back to the window and watched as a man lifted creels off the back of an open truck and stacked them with the others. The cages were empty.

The next morning a little dog was sitting by the front door. As soon as he saw Evie, he yelped and yapped.

'That's Keeper,' the receptionist said as Evie stroked the dog. 'He's one of the island dogs. Roams everywhere, he does.'

Keeper followed Evie and her mother to the beach, and while Evie threw crusts to the gulls the little dog ran after them, but the birds always snatched them away first. Evie and Ma ran along the sand, and then took off their sandals and paddled in the sea. Evie thought it was as if they were both children in a storybook about a family going on holiday to the seaside. Except, of course, she could not help feeling sad. The dog just stayed by the water's edge, quivering and barking.

At night Evie pulled Bunny in with her under the covers. Only when she was sure that Ma was asleep did she feel for the toy rabbit's neck and push her fingers inside the seam. Evie could feel the piece of paper, crunching beneath her fingers, reminding her of her promise. The note with the telephone number was inside Bunny's neck; she could smell the ink from the pen he had used. 'Call me,' he'd said. 'Promise, you'll ring. I'll be waiting.' And he had made a promise too, that if she called, he would not tell her Ma about what she had been doing.

He had been hiding at the bottom of the garden, beyond the apple tree – the area where the lawn was seldom mown. The shed had been abandoned a long time ago; it was rotten and no longer secure enough even for the garden tools. Evie cried out when she saw who it was in the shed, but he had put his hand over her mouth and kept it there until she was quiet. He began to kiss her, like he always did, in a harsh, greedy way, and Evie struggled to get away, but he kept one hand over her mouth and pressed down on her with his body. She could smell his breath, taste the rotten cigarettes, feel his sweat.

'You love me, don't you, Evie?' he said. 'Say you do. I won't hurt you, just say you love me.'

'Yes, yes,' she cried.

Ma was standing on a large rock on the tideline, and with every push of the waves, it became a temporary island. There was just enough room for both of them to stand on it. They saluted as if they were at the wheel of a great galleon. Evie was a sailor, and Ma a pirate.

'Walk the plank,' Evie commanded. The plank was just a ridge of rock that protruded above the sand, but Ma had to walk along and back again before the next wave arrived.

'I love this place!' Ma proclaimed when she was back to the safety of the large rock. Evie hugged Ma's legs so tight that she almost tipped her into the sea.

That night, Evie dreamed of her old house, the one they

had left behind. In the dream, she was looking through the window into her bedroom, but the window had bars across it. Evie could still see her dolls' house, her teaset, her collection of ponies, even their combs and brushes, and the gymkhana made from a box with a painted backdrop of lollipop trees with red circles for apples. She could see it all, but she could not touch them. She wanted to go inside, but she knew that he'd be angry if she did not go to him. So she ran to the end of the garden, and the door of the shed was open, and he was there, waiting, and his head turned towards her, his eyes all watery.

She woke up, her heart beating fast, she was sweating, and she did not know where she was at first. The room glowed with a yellow light. The street lamps flickered, and their light filtered through the striped curtains making shadowed lines on the wall, like bars. She could see the shape of Ma in the bed next to her; she could hear the sound of her breathing. She thought of all the times she had heard Ma crying and him shouting. She knew that Ma was safe here, but she must be sure; she must know that he would keep his promise. She listened to the footsteps outside and the voices too.

She thought about the lobsters in their crates, and she felt her throat tightening.

Evie crept down to the hallway. Keeper was there, looking sleepy, surprised. As she slipped into the phone booth, he nuzzled her leg and then sloped off towards Reception. Without turning on the light, Evie reached up and lifted the handset. Immediately, a voice came from the small holes of the receiver. 'Operator. What number please?'

Evie froze. She didn't have a number. She had left it inside Bunny.

'Hello, hello,' the voice continued. 'Operator service.'

Evie dropped the receiver, and it clunked against the wall. She opened the door and in front of her stood the receptionist. The woman seemed taller now, and behind her the stairs rising from the hallway were steeper, as if the shadows of the night had lengthened everything.

In the morning Ma looked into Evie's face. 'You've not slept well,' she said. 'I can tell.'

Evie said nothing. She did not speak all through breakfast. That day, Ma was first down the steps to the beach. The tide was already on its way out, and their island rock was completely exposed, surrounded by cold, wet sand.

'OK,' Ma said. 'What is it? You were so happy yesterday.'

At first, Evie tried not to speak, but the silence was too much, and its weight nudged at her until she thought she might cry. She was almost about to tell her mother about what happened in the shed, but she couldn't – something stopped her.

'Oh, Evie! Why?' Ma's voice had a sharp edge to it that reminded Evie of the sting of the wiry grass of the dunes when it cut her foot. As Evie looked at her, Ma's shoulders sank and then she was smiling again, but it was a thin smile that wavered at the edges of her mouth. 'Evie, darling. We have everything here, everything we could possibly need, and we can buy you new toys and clothes. We're safe here.'

Evie turned away from the sea and ran, first towards the cliffs, then along the pebble ridge that went along the top of the beach. The stones clattered beneath her feet, and as they fell down the bank, there was a hollow echo as if beneath her was a great hole. She could hear Ma calling, but she did not stop.

Ma caught up with her by the time they reached the hotel, but she was out of breath when she entered the lobby, wheezing.

'Oh, my!' exclaimed the woman at the desk. 'What a glorious day to be running with the wind behind you.'

Evie looked up and saw her toy rabbit, her Bunny, behind the counter, shoved into a place where the newspapers were kept.

'Bunny!' Evie shouted. 'My Bunny.'

Ma tutted. Evie shook Ma's hand from her shoulder.

'Yes, dearie,' the woman said. 'I noticed she could do with a stitch or two. The poor thing was falling apart at the seams.'

'Oh, that's very kind of you,' Ma said as the receptionist handed the toy rabbit to Evie.

Evie snatched the toy. She saw the new stitching around the neck, and she pulled the rabbit's head as hard as she could.

'Stop it,' Ma said. 'Stop it now, don't be so ungrateful.'

Ma pulled the rabbit too, clasping the body, but Evie would not let go. She still had hold of the head.

'I won't! I won't!' Evie shouted.

Ma lowered her voice to a whisper. 'Evie! Calm down.' Her words came out through her teeth like a hiss.

Evie was crying; the tears streamed down her face. Ma had an arm around her shoulders, and as she steered her away towards the lounge, she turned towards the receptionist. 'I'm so sorry; she's a little homesick.'

Once they had turned the corner and were through the doorway, Ma yanked at the toy, but Evie was not ready to let go. Instead, the rabbit's head was pulled cleanly from its body. The new stitches tore apart, and the stuffing was exposed. Only the fluff of kapok bulged from the broken neck. The piece of paper with the number on it had gone.

Down at the harbour, a new cache of lobster pots lined the quay, and from them came the aroma of sea and weed and deep, deep ocean. The men were below, out of sight, only their voices resounding as they hosed down the deck of a boat. Evie crouched in front of a cage, its captive moved weakly, exhausted as the tight weave of the creel would not allow it to escape. Evie knew what she must do.

She could see that it would not take much. She only had to tip the basket slightly and lift the catch. Before she thought about what it was she was releasing, the catch had snapped back; as if by intention only, she had opened a door, springing it wide open. The lobster clattered onto the quayside, rolled forward, unfurled its scissoring legs, pinching the air with its largest claw and reaching out towards Evie. She held back, pressed against the pile of creels with their live contents, and feeling a nip, she had no choice but to move towards the ugly crustacean, but by now it was scrabbling on the smooth, worn stones by the edge, and immediately it fell over the quayside into the sea.

'Away, away!' she shouted. 'Don't ever come back.'

The sound of Evie's voice carried on the wind, fleeting, dissipating with the outgoing tide.

A Taste for Blood

In the time before the recording of history, the world was a place of many trees, where forests swirled with mists, and amphibious creatures swam unheeded through the streams and rivers, leaping from pool to pool and wallowing in the deepest lakes. There was an abundance of vegetation and many kinds of animals that grazed and multiplied. There were the Stick People, too. It was said that they had come from the trees because of their long slender sapling-like limbs, and their skin was as rough as old bark. They had everything they needed and never had to go far for food or drink; their shelters were the weather-hewn caves of the soft rocky cliffs, and their natural resting places were carved into the trees. They spent their days lolling in the moss, paddling their canoes in the shallows, teasing the fish by tickling their gills. They climbed along the overhanging boughs until the slim branches swayed and bowed and could no longer hold their weight, at which point they hollered and lurched into the deep pools sending wave upon wave rippling towards the far green banks.

Adam is reading from the *Book of Stories* as Dawn surveys the kitchen. Play-Doh in lumps on the kitchen table, the floor is marked with the tread of small human footprints. Adam is on the sofa in the corner of the room, leaning back, his legs crossed one over the other. Jethro is next to him in his pyjamas, nudging him to continue, pointing at the pictures. Adam takes a sip of wine from the glass at his side, looks up, and smiles at Dawn. She turns back to the sink where the washing up bowl is filled to the brim with bubbles that glisten and reflect the light from the window making colourful rhomboids on the walls. She pushes her hands into the froth to retrieve the toys.

Earlier on, she felt relieved when Carly had come to collect Alex. It had not been an easy day. Dawn had left the two three-year-olds only for a few moments while she answered the phone – they were building a tower of bricks in the living room. She had heard the rise and fall of their voices from the hallway as she listened to the electronic message coming through the receiver – another call from the Council's rent collection arrears department. Then – crash! A scream.

Dawn dropped the phone and ran back to the living room. The floor was covered with the scattered remains of the demolished tower, and Alex was throwing bricks at Jethro who just stood there, quite still, as each brick bounced off his head. He was not even crying. Dawn grabbed Alex's arm just as he was about to throw a small wooden hammer at the television screen.

She had managed the situation well, Dawn mused, but things had come to a bitter end later on while the two boys were making animals out of matchsticks and plasticine. There were not enough matchsticks, so she had added a few cocktail sticks – that was the mistake. Cocktail sticks are weapons – they have sharp pointy ends that hurt when stabbed into flesh. Dawn could not collect them in quickly enough once she realised her error. Alex had shoved a cocktail stick at Jethro's face, just missing his eye.

When Carly had phoned the previous day to ask if she would have Alex, Dawn had hesitated. It will be good for Alex and Jethro, Carly explained, it will give them the opportunity to make up for their recent falling-out. Not very diplomatic, Dawn thought, but she agreed to look after Alex. Carly had been having a difficult time lately: her partner, not the father of Alex, had left her. She'd never liked Chas because of how he was with Alex – too strict and unaware of how unhappy it made Alex. And now Carly had an appointment at the hospital to check a lump in her breast that was probably a cyst – but there was always that worry. Naturally, Dawn wanted to help out.

Dawn lifts out the bright plastic toys from the bubbles: shape moulds, cutters, rollers, and a large dice. It reminds her of a lucky dip, but one where you'd get another chance if you weren't pleased with the gift. Dawn rinses each item under the tap and leaves them to dry on the draining board. Behind her, Adam clears his throat and carries on with the story.

The Stick People had never known hunger, but one day, when they were bored, they set out to chase the creatures of the forest – for sport at first – but then they began to kill them. They were beautiful creatures, untamed but gentle: deer, hogs, wildcats, and crows. The Stick People wondered what to do with their freshly killed victims, and it was not long before they developed a taste for blood.

'Eurgh!' Jethro exclaims in horror and delight.
    'What is this story?' Dawn asks, with a concerned look. 'Are you sure it's suitable for a three-year-old?'
    'Don't stop, don't stop!' Jethro urges.

The Stick People became greedy, and rather than take what they needed, they slaughtered more and more of the fauna of the forest, not even bothering to save or salt the leftovers. They had no idea that one day there would be a dearth of flesh. The problems began because many of the creatures they slaughtered were young, and had not yet had the chance to reproduce. Inevitably, when their favourite source of food was scarce, the Stick People became restless and discontented. It was getting harder and harder to put meat on the stone tables, and they began to steal hunks and slithers from each other's abodes, often in the dark of the night, which resulted in many firelight fights where the loser would end up singed, or worse – burnt to a cinder.

Carly said that Alex had been up since five o'clock that morning, and he certainly looked tired when they arrived. Rather than walk with them to the playgroup, Dawn strapped the two infants into the double buggy she'd borrowed from her neighbour. On the way home, they went to the park and spent ten minutes playing on the slide. Dawn hoped that they would be tired out, and that after lunch the boys would both have a nice long nap – but it was not to be. Before they reached home the trouble started. The two boys began elbowing each other in the buggy, followed by Alex digging his fingers into the flesh of Jethro's arm. They had not far to go so Dawn walked as fast as she could, pushing the loaded buggy up the hill. They had just rounded the last corner when Jethro screamed. Alex had grabbed at the flesh of Jethro's cheek and would not let go. Dawn stopped, pushed on the brake, and, with considerable effort, prised open Alex's hand. She undid the harness and pulled her sobbing son out of the buggy, giving him, the injured one, all the attention. Dawn was seething with anger at Alex, but she tried not to show it – she told herself that he was only three years old, to keep calm, and remember the advice she'd read in her book on good child-rearing.

'Let's get you both home,' Dawn said in a false-calm voice.

'He hurt me,' Jethro sobbed.

'It was him!' Alex shouted, even though the evidence was not on his side.

'Don't tell tales, Alex,' Dawn snapped.

She had felt her anger rising. And then she repeated the words, louder. Here she was, shouting at a small child in the street. She even stamped her foot on the ground.

Dawn picked out the cocktail sticks from the bottom of the bowl, catching one with her fingernail. The pain was greater than she would have expected, but the only sign of injury was a tiny spot of blood under the nail. She put her finger in her mouth and sucked until her finger was white.

The old gods of the forest watched and wept from the canopies; they knew there was nothing they could do to stop the Stick People from destroying the creatures of the forest. Eventually, when all the animals were extinct, and the people no longer had the strength to fight each other, they went back to eating the leaves of the trees and the many plants that carpeted the forest floors; cracking the nuts and eating the kernels, collecting berries in the autumn, and making a red tar that could be stored and used in winter soups. Sometimes they even collected the bitter weeds that floated in the pools, and cooked them up to make a stinking, green broth. The population of the Stick People decreased, not through lack of nutrition, but because of all the slaughtering they had done, and there were still random fights over scraps of mouse meat.

Carly was always going on about parents who fed their children 'crap', and how easy it was to provide a healthy diet. Dawn could hear Carly's voice in her head: 'You just have to get into a routine of baking your own bread and making purées from organic fruit and vegetables. Then you can freeze them, so that you always have something nutritious to hand.'

Dawn had kept quiet, and felt guilty about feeding Jethro processed foods: fish fingers, baked beans, corn from a tin, and cottage cheese with pineapple bits – his favourite. It wasn't that Dawn didn't care about giving her child healthy food, she liked to do other things too – playing games and going to the park, or taking little trips on the bus or train – rather than staying at home to prepare a perfect three-course mini-lunch.

The drone of Adam's reading voice broke through the murmur of her thoughts. Dear Adam. He was a good friend. He had been holding a bottle of wine when she answered the door to him. 'It's local,' he declared, 'from a vineyard over Southwoods way.' He looked a little nervous standing there in his green trousers, his smock top and the little round hat that he always wore. 'And I found a storybook for Jethro, too. It has lots of wacky pictures I thought he might like.'

When they had walked through to the kitchen from the front door, Alex, who was strapped into Jethro's old highchair, had tears streaming down his face. His bowl of food was tipped upside down on the floor, and on the tray in front of him was the stick hedgehog that Jethro had made earlier, the one with sharp cocktail sticks protruding from its body. Jethro was smiling. He was sitting at the table and it sounded as if he was counting, not in numbers, but in made-up words. With each count, he pulled up a length of spaghetti, and turning his head sideways, he slurped it into his mouth. Alex had stopped crying and was staring at Jethro as he sucked up each wiggly string.

New folk arrived from beyond the windy valleys and the stormy highlands. They brought with them seeds and beans and pulses, which they offered in exchange for the wooden items of the Stick People. Partly through fear, partly through curiosity. The Stick People took against them and hid at first, but then they caught the new folk in an ambush and threw stones at them. But the new folk were stronger. They overwhelmed the Stick People, took away their mallets, cart wheels and carved signs. The words of the Travelling Folk were spoken in a tongue that made no sense to the Stick People, but they soon learned to chant the sounds over and over.

The Stick People and the Travelling Folk settled down together, and learned how to grow edible roots and climbing beans; they discovered how some plants grew more profusely if they were planted next to the trees, clinging on to them for support, and how others thrived in the open clearings. After many seasons, the New Stick People had perfected their agricultural arts and were able to produce enough food for everyone. Their children, who were the grandchildren and great-grandchildren of the lolling meat-eaters, grew up having never seen a live animal, and if they were to, it would not have occurred to them to eat the meat of a beast or the bony flesh of a fish. Their only knowledge of these creatures came from cave drawings and the tales told by their grandparents.

Jethro pointed to the stick-like characters; some were climbing the trees, some building houses or towers – others were fighting. Once Dawn had finished clearing up the kitchen, she sank onto the sofa next to Adam and Jethro. She sipped her glass of wine, and her mind drifted away with Adam's voice in the background reading the last chapter of the strange old story of the Stick People. Jethro snuggled up between them, curling into the curves of her body while she kissed his bruised forehead.

As they grew up, the youngsters wanted more from life; they wanted to travel and explore, to find new places that would take them to worlds beyond their imaginations; they wanted a future filled with rainbows. They asked the elders about life in the forests, but the elders knew only the tales that were the memories the old folk that had been passed from the generations before –

the stories of dearth and death. But the youngsters were curious, and once the desire for knowledge had eaten into them, they could not leave it alone.

The elders whispered their stories into the ears of the youngsters, filling their thoughts with rainbows that shimmered with images of the land of their ancestors. The young people drifted into a dreamy sleep, and when they awoke, they yearned for the cool of the trees and the deep forests and began to chant the rhymes and the half-remembered verses they had heard in their dreams.

Gestation

Hestor's necklace glows orange, warmed by her flesh as it nests within the shelf of her clavicle. The amber beads are a gift, which had been passed on from her grandmother to her mother, and from her mother to Hestor.

The conversation around the dinner table drifts into the everyday – cars, food, shoes, clothes, travel. Everything is fine. So far. And then the conversation turns to children, and wakeful nights and babies. Hestor is silent. But the woman at her side persists. Hestor takes a deep breath. Sleep deprivation – a safe enough subject as, these days, Hestor is mostly nocturnal – so she talks about her neighbours' dog, the one that is kept in a kennel outside and barks throughout the night. She prefers cats, she says. Her old, black tabby has a special place in her heart. All is fine until the woman tells how she and her husband gave their daughter the gift of a kitten as compensation for the arrival of another baby in the family.

'I sometimes think we're better off without them,' the woman continues. 'Children, of course, but I cannot imagine being without them.' She is looking directly at Hestor.

Hestor's hand plucks at the fulgid buds of her necklace.

Later, when Hestor is alone, she undresses. Firstly, she unclips the necklace. She holds the beads up to the light of the moon and watches as they sway like a pendulum. They have a regular rhythm at first, but then that slows and slows until the motion is barely discernible. Now, they lay cold and heavy in her hands.

But she has seen the lunar shine through each bead, and how, within each nugget, life has been revealed. A speck within each bead, where every dark fleck has sections: a tiny head, an abdomen, legs, wings – these lives have been suspended in a nub of amber.

She takes the necklace to the dressing table, and with a pair of sharp nail scissors, she cuts the thread between each bead, letting them drop one at a time. Then she takes a single bead and places it into her mouth, letting it warm on her tongue. As each sealed cell melts, she feels the flutter.

The Intercession

He has mown the grass around the gravestones, tended the small kitchen garden where he grows runner beans, shallots, and carrots, tightened the string ties across the beds to keep away the gulls and crows. And all with the use of his one good arm. He has no name, and he hardly speaks to a soul. He has been here for thirty years as a warden, but no one remembers how he came to be here, or from where he arrived. The church congregation and the minister are used to him and his quiet ways – this man who speaks to no one. On summer evenings, he can be found seated in a rocking chair on the narrow veranda at the back of the presbytery, staring into the dusk, perhaps watching the blue butterflies perform their final dance around the flowering gorse.

This evening is no different – except that there is a storm brewing out to sea. Dark clouds are gathering on the horizon, moving closer to shore. The ocean waters are rising, rolling along the surface, waves folding in tighter and tighter curls.

On 12 August 1944, the inhabitants of the island of Sarsenne were aroused from their slumbers. The distant firing of guns on the mainland had hardly impinged on their lives during the last couple of months. The sound was carried on the wind and diminished into a boom like an irregular heartbeat. It was four in the morning when the Home Guards came, calling from house to house, advising everyone to evacuate the island. The enemy had been seen. Vessels of war were speeding towards the shore. There was no time to ponder over which items to take or leave behind. Parents woke their children, lifting them from their beds still tangled in their blankets. They pulled out suitcases that had long lain gathering dust on the tops of wardrobes, and stuffed them with whatever came to hand. Anything they could not take that they considered to be valuable was hidden away or buried in their gardens. These mounds of freshly dug soil would later be kicked over and their treasures looted. Cats and dogs were fed; poultry and cattle were turned out of their stalls and left to the mercy of the invaders.

The young priest, Fr Petrus, knelt in front of his altar at the church of St Agnes and prayed. He was the most recent incumbent in a long line of priests, most of whom had stayed in post until their dying day. For generations, the church had been a source of comfort and courage to the inhabitants and, in return for spiritual protection, had grown wealthy. After all, the livelihoods of the Islanders came from the rich pickings of the sea. They believed that it was through the intercession of the priest that the seas around them continued to be replenished.

The church community had gathered on the previous evening to prepare for the next day's special service. They had brought flowers, baskets burgeoning with fruit, and boxes of produce overlaid with fresh herbs: rosemary, sage, chamomile. The altar was laid out in a profusion of colour and scents. The priest sighed, took a nervous breath and said a prayer to St Agnes. He knew that if she had been there, she would have stayed and faced the enemy as once she had thwarted the Lions of Rome and the burning flames of the witch's fire. Fr Petrus trembled and prayed for strength. In return for his deliverance to safety, he promised the saint that he would return to her namesake church.

The reliquary casket had seldom been opened; in fact never, to the knowledge of Fr Petrus. Now, here he was, pushing the filigreed key into the lock, his hands shaking as he muttered and maundered his devotions. He was surprised when the key slipped easily into the lock, and thought that perhaps the saint was by his side. He turned the key anti-clockwise until he heard the clunk. With the casket open, the scent of incense wafted out, and Fr Petrus reached into the velvet lining to find the box with the relic. It was a plain box, considering it was housed in a silver and gold casket, with a simple cross carved into the lid. This relic was believed to be a single bone, a phalanx, from the finger of St Agnes. It had been on the island since 1461, when the boat in which the relic was being transported foundered on the rocks at low tide. The priests who were responsible for its transportation swam to the shore with the relic wrapped and sealed inside the box. A casket was later commissioned and paid for by the Islanders. With the relic safely and luxuriously housed, it had been installed before the altar of a side chapel designated to St Agnes. Now the relic would be taken on another journey.

Fr Petrus slipped the key into his pocket and made his way to the door, turning just once to genuflect before walking down to the pier, the wooden box under his arm. Fr Petrus left on the final boat. As he watched the harbour shrinking into the distance and the island flag twisting around its pole, he prayed to St Agnes and begged for her intercession. In return, he promised that he would take care of the last of her mortal remains and to restore it to its rightful resting place if only his life could be spared. But his prayer was caught by the wind and tossed across the ocean.

A great storm brewed, and the boat was pitched from side to side, lifted by the swell, pulled back and forth until it was filled with the spume of the overlapping waves. All hands were on deck, every bailer to hand, but it was useless. Even when the storm passed, as soon as the hull emptied, it quickly refilled, sinking slowly, until eventually, it was barely afloat. By now, the boat had become separated from the convoy, but still it limped along with the pull of the tide, all the time sinking further and further until the captain gave the orders to abandon ship.

By now they were into enemy waters, and the in-going tide was pulling them back towards Sarsenne. It would do them no good to send up the flares. The reputation of the enemy, with its vile punishments, threatened a fate worse than drowning. They would take their chances. Even the slight mercy of the cold sea was preferable to the embrace of a vicious enemy. The women and children were ushered into the lifeboats, and the crew swung themselves in after them, calling to Fr Petrus to do the same. But the boat pitched and creaked, and the lifeboats drifted away leaving Fr Petrus, a silhouette of a priest, standing at the bow, praying for intercession, his rosary in his hands.

He knew what he must do: he took hold of the one remaining lifebelt and pushed it around the wooden chest. Then he threw everything he held into the swirling water before launching himself overboard. It was only a few seconds later, when the boat upended, heading down and down towards the seabed, Fr Petrus surfaced, gulping in the air as he came up and plunged down over and over, only to rise again. Once he had gained enough breath, he cried out for help, but there was no helping hand, no guardian angel who came to pluck him from the sea. Instead, the wooden chest hooped by the lifebelt appeared in front of him. He flung himself towards it, and when he had caught it he was determined not to lose it, so he pushed one arm between it and the lifebelt. Despite the cold water, his arm began to swell, and the pressure was like the squeezing of a tourniquet. There he remained on the surface of the sea, a human rudder to a small wooden chest.

But the sea was filling with flotsam rising from the sinking boat. A body floated by, the head uppermost, long hair swirling like the tentacles of a strange sea creature. He watched, muttering his incantations, mesmerised, almost forgetting his predicament. The wooden planks of the dismembered boat sprung to the surface, and a shaft of mast came up from behind him. A sudden wave dashed it against his head sending him under the water and throwing him into darkness.

Fr Petrus knew nothing more until he heard waves crashing onto shingle and felt them pounding at the rawness of his body. He looked across and saw his arm, blue and stiff, still anchored to the wooden box. He had been thrown onto a beach of tiny stones and shells, a place he did not recognise, unmapped for all he knew, and for an unknown time he lay there. Then there came the sound of crushing shingle, becoming louder; there were footsteps moving towards him. Through his blinkered vision, he saw a pair of feet, and heard a child's voice, or was it a woman's voice – or could it be an angel's? He tried to look up, but the light was blinding him. He could not make out what or who it was, and then he realised. Only a halo could be this bright, the halo of a saint. He thought she smiled as she bent towards him but he felt nothing as the box was pulled free of his arm and the life belt. The vision was disappearing, moving away, the bright light diminishing, and all he felt was the spray of small stones from the retreating heels. He shivered violently and passed into oblivion.

❦

The warden genuflects in front of the altar. He will tidy away the hymnals and missals now that Evensong has passed and the congregation dismissed. He is alone, and all is quiet, almost. He lingers for a moment, listening. Then from somewhere behind him is a thwack. A dropping latch. The chime of iron on iron has his heart lurching. He lifts his head and looks towards the door. The ring handle is turning as if closing. He looks back to the altar and sees that a corner of embroidered cloth is lifting in the slight draught. Right in the centre is a small wooden chest. He is sure that it was not there before. He had watched the priest tidy away the accoutrements of communion. Still knelt on his one knee of genuflection, he arises awkwardly, then moves towards the altar, in fear, his arms held wide as if to tame a wild animal.

He feels the sides of the box. It is a simple box, but roughened with age and swollen, as if it has emerged from the water. It is firmly closed, locked tight, and he cannot prise it open with his thumbs. He feels over the raised letters on the lid that stand proud of the distended wood. He speaks the name: St Agnes. Carefully, he lifts the small chest and takes it with him to the vestry. He remembers there is a small key kept in the corner cabinet. He has never known where it has come from, but now he believes he has found the lock into which it fits. As he enters the vestry, he sees through the latticed window that the chain on the gate outside is swinging.

He pushes the ornate key into the lock and, despite the crunch of grit and salt, it turns quite easily. Inside is a small bundle, a cloth wrapped tightly around it like a tiny Egyptian mummy, bleached and faded. The lights flicker momentarily as a crash of thunder strikes the land around the church. Grains of sand spill out as he pulls away at the rotten layers, unwinding the cloth until the contents are revealed – a tiny piece of bone – the phalanx of a saint. St Agnes has returned. Now he, Fr Petrus, knows, and he remembers his promise. He will return to the island of Sarsenne – with the last fragment of a mortal saint.

The Dissonance

At first glance, the manikins emerging from a crevice in the belfry look to be quite merry, but the sweet clavichordial tones of the bells belie them. Their faces are red, their grins toothless. Their clothes appear well-worn, and their limbs daubed with unmatched shades of paint. Even the cooper, bent over his barrel, head turned to one side, stares out bleakly as if he'd rather be anywhere else but imprisoned in the clock tower of *Ville St Ronan*. His demeanour is that of a weary man, so fatigued that only his cask keeps him upright. Next, comes a woman wearing a mob cap and an apron. Over her arm is what was once a basket of flowers, but it now looks more like a limp animal at her side. And the maid that follows has her arm broken off at the wrist – it once held a jug of beer – but she no longer fills the tankards of her kinsfolk with cheer. Perhaps she has had enough of the monkey that pursues her with his grotesque visage and his leery jeer. The most disturbing figurine of all is the skeleton: bones screeching on a rickety frame, one leg sundered below the knee, and in his hand, he holds a scythe. His head is cocked to the side as if listening for the final throes of an unsuspecting client. These mannequins are purportedly the re-creation of the townspeople of *St Ronan* from a previous century. As dramatis personae, they are preserved, forced to act out their scene, day-in, day-out – a reminder to the present incumbents of the role of citizen that they are the descendants who will one day also be doomed to count the passage of time.

As the motley characters move from right to left along the track at the base of the glockenspiel clock, their feet fixed in perpetuity to the metal rail, the rattle and the squeak of the un-oiled and poorly maintained mechanism should herald a warning.

Today, *Le Petit Jardin* is the first shop to open; its shutters unleashed by a young woman called Lili, a student who works at the flower shop every Saturday. The first sound to greet the ears of the other shopworkers and early morning passers-by is a metallic creak and a rush of the metal roller as it is raised. The tobacconist, the boutique owner, and the two brothers who run the café are on their way to the cluster of shops in the town's main square, the *Place de l'Horloge*. As they pass by, they call out their greetings to Lili.

Soon the streets will be adorned with tables dressed in fresh linen; parasols fixed to their heavy bases, matching chairs wiped clean. There will be artificial trees in pots placed at discreet intervals and linked ropes to demarcate the cafés, and an array of signage scribed in an archaic script denoting the 'olde worlde' atmosphere. Lili uses the hooked end of the pole to catch hold of the metal hoop of the canopy. She draws the striped awning out and over the pavement. It is her job to sweep the paving stones at the front of the shop, to mop away the excretions of the previous night, when the enthusiastic drinkers stain the pavement with their vomit and piss. Lili gags, and stretches the collar of her shirt, pulling it up over her mouth.

Madame Fleuriste will be arriving soon with fresh flowers from the market, and she will not be pleased if the shop has not been prepared, especially today, on the 500th anniversary of the Great Fire. It was a fire that purged the town, cremating many and leaving in its wake the decimated shells of the original buildings. Despite all this, the town soon rose from the ashes like the proverbial phoenix. Nowadays, there is only one building that has survived from the time before the Great Fire – the old clock tower. There is a story, an old wives' tale perhaps, that should the clock ever stop then a terrible visitation will descend upon the inhabitants. Of course, no one takes this seriously these days, and in truth, the annual celebration is mainly held for mercurial reasons rather than a serious cultural revival. In any case, the festival is successful enough for the town's businesses to invest a little extra energy, resources and time. Madame Fleuriste is one of the hosts who embraces the festival, making the most of its opportunities.

Now she has arrived at *Le Petit Jardin*. She is flustered, her trolley loaded with an abundance of colourful blooms, some already wilting. She has had to park her car several streets away as the road closure restrictions have been in force since midnight. She is waving her hand at Lili, giving her instructions to unload the flowers and place them in fresh water. She is sweating profusely, her satin dress already marked with patches of perspiration, wisps of dark hair loosening from her chignon. Lili fetches a glass of cold milk from the fridge in the back, but even that does not dissolve the agitated spirit of her employer, who is tutting and moving the pots and buckets that Lili has carefully placed out on the pavement at the front of the shop.

Lili's first job is to make up the gift packs of tiny bouquets in the colours of the day: red and orange to denote the flames. Lili has precise instructions. She must make up thirty miniature bouquets that consist of a fern, a sprig of gypsophila and a single spray of yellow jasmine, and all wrapped in orange and red tissue paper snipped at the ends in a flame-like array. She must – and this is important – add a business card with the details of *Le Petit Jardin* into the paper folds. These posies are to be given out to each passer-by with the intention of enticing them, via the musky aroma of the jasmine-scented bouquet, into the cool interior of the florist.

Lili winds her way through the crowd handing out the tiny bouquets. Everyone is delighted and is smiling, despite the discomfort of the heat. The atmosphere is that of a carnival: the music of the *Ville St Ronan* brass band, a jester cavorting in medieval costume, jugglers spinning their clubs into the air, a town crier ringing a handbell, a procession of pipers in sequinned masks and feathered caps loop their way around the cafés. There is even a fire-eater who looks as if he might extinguish the flames with his sweat. Flags lag heavily from tall poles in the humid air. Official guides offer tours of the town in a variety of languages. But the longest queue is for the ice cream vendor who is selling the famous *la crème glacée du feu* – the bright cream stripes denote the colours of the flames of the Great Fire.

The sun is high in the sky, and it would not be unreasonable to think that the temperature is almost equivalent to that of the great fire itself. One could imagine the ghostly flames lapping at the legs of the pedestrians. But, despite the heat, many are still happy to venture out into the midday sun. Many pink-faced tourists have spent the morning browsing the antique markets that run along the back streets, and some have come to the *Place de l'Horloge* to sit in the partial shade on the far side of the town hall. Others outstay their welcome at one the cafés – much to the annoyance of many a maître d' who persists in asking if they would like another drink, or perhaps they would like the bill.

Lili has given out all the bunches of flowers, and she joins the queue that has formed below the clock tower. She knows that she should return to the shop, but Lili is out of sight, and later she will find an excuse to give Madame Fleuriste – she feels she deserves a break after all. An ice cream will cool her down, and anyway she won't have long to wait – she knows the lad who serves the ice cream.

The musicians have finished their last number, and it is not long before they have packed away their instruments and are making their way out of the town square. For a moment, all is quiet except for the muttering of voices from the people in the queue. But then the languid murmurs are raised, some are whispers, becoming a little louder, and the excited voices of children fill the air. Everyone looks up. It is a few minutes before midday – the time when the clock delivers its famous signature. The mechanism begins creaking into action, and soon the first bells are chiming, heralding the appearance of the figurines: the cooper with his barrel, the flower-seller, followed by the girl, then the monkey, and, finally, the skeleton. It is just when the girl is tilting on her hinge, about to be drawn feet-first through the coffin-like exit, that it happens.

All eyes are watching as the skeleton takes centre-stage. The clock creaks a little more; then it rattles as if the cogs are straining to turn, pressing onto the back of Time, as if urging it not to stop. There is a judder, the bells are clanging one against the other in discordance, until finally they are stilled. The figurine of the girl is lying on her side, and the monkey has drooped as if about to fold over. Only the skeleton is upright, albeit, with a crooked demeanour, cheekbones lifted above its hollow face in an eerie grimace.

Lili feels a spit of cold fear; it makes her shiver, despite the heat.

The skeleton shakes as if to reassemble its parts, or

perhaps to bring its bones back to life. The hand with the scythe lifts as if it is about to deal a deathly blow. But the cogs are resisting. A mechanical screech is followed by an ear-splitting whistle, more like a wail. The hands of the clock – the hour-hand and the minute-hand – drop, simultaneously, as if the bolt that has fastened them to the centre of the clock has finally lost its hold. From their heavenward position, the hands swing down and, for a moment, they sway until they both stop at the six, their arrow-like ends pointing directly at the line of people below them – the queue for *la crème glacée du feu*.

'Vite!' Lili shouts, and to the people all around her, 'Everyone run, run away!'

But nobody moves, it is as if no one has heard her. But then neither does she move. Lili's eyes are fixed on the clock tower. The skeleton continues to stare straight ahead from his great height, as if surveying the entire town, taking in its old boundaries, its streets, the way the buildings and the roads continue into the valleys, extending over the furthest hills in a sprawling urban city. The hand with the scythe is still raised, but the head of the skeleton drops, clicking from the neck. The adults are looking up at him; some are pointing, the children are laughing.

From within the great tower, a single bell rings, and the creak of wheels and cogs can be heard juddering and whirring into action. The clock's hands begin to move again, slowly at first, and then like a spring that has been pulled to its full extent, primed for action and then released – the hands swing and whirl around the clock face, regaining the seconds, making up the lost minutes, until they reach their midday position. And only then does the skeleton lower his scythe and resume his position in the line, sliding along the rail in a relentless parade. Ripples of delight run through the crowd. And from the depths of the clock tower can be heard the carillon of cast bronze bells jangling a cacophonous, dissonant sound.

A Wake in the Water

Customs had been awkward. They'd insisted that Graham opened up the back of the lorry. Fortunately, he hadn't had to unpack everything, just open a box or two, but it had taken up time, and he was tired after the drive. They'd asked him lots of questions. He must have looked nervous to be picked out like that, and, to be fair, he felt nervous. It was a very long time since he'd been on a ferry, forty years to be precise, but this was the Channel, not the Irish Sea.

He was ten years old on that last trip, when they'd gone on holiday to the Isle of Man. His mother had wanted them to have a special holiday, as a family. Most years, they only went on day trips. It was because of the business, his father claimed. But his mother had heard how beautiful the island was, and talked about the gardens and the castles, and how she longed to pay a visit. But Father only agreed to go with them on day trips, later in the summer, and only to the usual places: Crosby, or Lytham St Annes. There had been arguments at home about the 'big' holiday.

'It's only for a week,' Mother said. 'Surely the business won't collapse in that time.'

And anyway, they had Mikey. He'd look after it, keep the shop open, and make sure that everything ticked over. But Father disagreed. He could not trust Mikey; even though Mikey had worked for him for seven years, he would not leave him in charge.

Then Mother became ill, and the doctor had said that a holiday would do her the world of good. She'd be able to come home refreshed and ready for the treatment. Father had had to agree.

Graham's old job meant that he drove from depot to warehouse or warehouse to retail outlet and back again, all within the UK, and mostly within the same day. But now that the company had been taken over by a multinational group there would be no more cruising up and down the motorways of Britain in the wee small hours, or pootling along the A roads, reversing into factory compounds, or edging skilfully down a narrow track to the back entrance of a shop. This trip was his first major trans-European job, and he'd been asked to collect a consignment from Lithuania.

The other truckers had gone to the cafeteria for a greasy breakfast and a mug of deep brown tea. Graham knew that his stomach would not cope with it at this time of night, so he went straight to the bar. A slug of whisky would be the best way to calm his jitters. And then another. He already felt a little woozy, and they had not yet left the port. Some fresh air would help. So he made his way up to the open deck by way of the narrow metal stairway. He arrived on the mid-deck, walked over to the railings, looked down at the murky waves lapping at the side of the hull, and watched them disappearing into the dark night.

The horn sounded three times, and with little more than a brief shunt, they glided out of the brightly lit harbour. Soon the reflections of the ship's lanterns were all that glittered on the swaying waves.

He walked towards the bow so he could look out from both sides of the boat. From the starboard, he watched the distant shore fading, lights diminishing, the cliffs receding into a ghostly wash. On the port side, the sea stretched out as black as the starless night. As the ferry turned to face the open sea, he could hear the waves slapping against the hull, racing alongside, before turning into a slim white wake. As he looked down, he watched the water and the rippling curls forming diagonal lines as the ferry moved forward. He became mesmerised. It calmed him, and he forgot his fear for a moment until something below him caught his attention.

He was sure he saw something in the water, something other than the coasting waves. Whatever it was, the wash quickly covered it over. Perhaps it was a dolphin playing in the foam. He had heard that dolphins often followed the boats, leaping across the wake or pushing up front to the bow of the boat, vying with each other to be the front-runner, or forming a line of mammalian-like tug boats, to lead the way. But this was no shoal, no school of dolphins, just a single one, a loner, and it wasn't leaping at all. There is was again. And it appeared with each lap of the waves before sinking into the black depths. Graham steadied himself against the rail and tried to be ready, to look closer the next time it surfaced.

He felt a prickle along his spine. He thought it was a head. Now he was sure. He was looking at a face, a human face, and not only that, there was something familiar about it, but he could not, at first, place it. As it bobbed up with the next wash of the wake, he noticed the cheekbones and the way the cropped hair exposed the ears. The face slipped under the water before he could get a closer look, and he strained to keep his eyes on the place where it went Sure enough, it reappeared again as the next line of wake-water pushed forward.

The eyes with their unblinking stare were looking up at him. A strange look, a look of knowing.

Graham checked behind him. He was alone. The other passengers were still inside, and he could hear the rumble of their voices, laughter, the cut of cutlery on plates, the clink of glass in the distance. But he could hear something else too, but it wasn't from inside the cabin. It came from the stillness of the night, from beyond the boat. He could hear a single voice.

He shivered, pulled up his collar, and closed the flaps of his jacket over his chest. He took in a deep breath, closed his eyes, just for a second, and opened them quickly as if to surprise the onlooker, the starer. But the face was still there, a man's face. The gaze of the eyes turned towards his, and the mouth agape was moving. He could even see the shape of the word as it formed, the way the mouth opened wide on the first syllable, followed by the lips closing over the teeth. Repeating the word over and over. Now he could hear the sound, albeit faint, and he knew what it was; the face was calling his name.

He grabbed the rail just as the rain began to fall. Huge droplets smacked down on the back of his head, running down his neck, into his clothes. He gulped at the air, let out a bellow, opened his mouth to the sky as if wanting it to fill with the rainwater. He swallowed hard, but all that filled his mouth was the bitter reflux, the acid taste of whisky, and he retched over the side.

🍃

From his child's-eye view, the ferry seemed huge from the harbour side, but once they were on board, his awe had diminished. On that day, too, the sea had been calm when they left the harbour, but a storm had quickly built up – it was not unusual, he learned afterwards, for the Irish Sea. Soon they were right out in the bay, and the boat was beginning to roll from side to side. People were pointing to the horizon where black clouds had gathered; others were hunched over the railings. He enjoyed the feeling of swaying from side to side as he ran onto the open deck and looked down from the rail. It was thrilling, just him and the sea and the wind and the boat. It was dangerous and exciting all at once, and there was nothing but his grip to stop him being swept out into the treacherous waters.

Numbed by the cold spray and deafened by the wind, he had forgotten about his parents until he felt the cuff to his ear and his arm wrenched away from the rail. His father's face was full of anger, as unpredictable as the sea. His moods were like that of the violent storm that had flickered into life from a cloud-filled, but seemingly placid, sky, forever brooding, broken by explosions that fell with a lightning force, hitting out in his fury at anyone who got in his way.

Graham wrenched himself away from his father's grip and ran away at the next violent roll. His slight body was now at the mercy of the wind, being pushed one way and then the other with every roll of the bucking ship. By now the waves had reached the full height of the boat, and were beginning to break over the bow. A flash of white water spilled onto the deck and ran over Graham's legs, tugging at his ankles.

People were slipping and falling over with the tilt of the ship, some were grabbing at the metal rungs, pulling open heavy iron hatchways and disappearing into the belly of the ship. Graham could no longer see his father. But he kept looking and calling. The waves were coming thicker and faster, and the next wave was already breaking and tipping right over the bow even before the previous wave had spilled out the other side. The boat lurched forward and down into the dip before the next wave towards the devouring sea.

A siren seared the air.

'Man overboard,' a voice on the Tannoy announced. 'Man overboard.'

The ship's engine began to grind, the deep throttle of the mechanism halting the forward motion of the ship. With the sting of the next wave, Graham was lifted off his feet, gulping and swallowing seawater as a wave washed over him and swept him backwards into the arms of two passengers who held tightly on to him.

❦

Now here he was again, on a ferry, but it was forty years later and this time it was different. The day before, he had gone to visit his mother, and she'd made him promise that he would return. He had told her that she need not fear, and that all would be well, that those kind of things never happened twice in a lifetime. In any case, it was a calm sea and the forecast was that it would remain so.

Now, the ship juddered and creaked across the sea, heading slowly into a moonless, clear night. Below him was water, miles and miles of deep salty water. Nothing else. He looked at his hands. Still grasping onto the rail, they had become icy cold, and along the skin of his knuckles he could see each white bone, and he realised that he had been holding on very tight, as if for his life. He let go. Nothing happened.

They were a long way out of the harbour, way beyond the curve of the great bay. He rubbed his hands together, bending his knees to steady his feet as the ship began to roll. He looked down from the deck. The face in the wake had gone, the stream of wash had become a ripple so faint that it hardly existed.

A Shift of Light

On the door to the living room was a map of the world. Bart hovered in front of it – push-pin in hand. The map already had several coloured pin-heads strewn across its land mass.

'Are you playing pin the tail on the donkey?' she asked.

'The secret to a good holiday is research,' Bart said, ignoring Dorla's flippant remark. 'The more you know about a place, the more successful the vacation.'

Bart was distracted from his map as Dorla tried on the Roman sandals she had bought from the open market earlier that day. While she crisscrossed the leather thongs around her calves, she knew that he would be irritated by them, particularly their lack of symmetry, but she ignored his frown and carried on.

'I want to go somewhere that's full of life, a place with markets, antique stalls, somewhere olde worlde,' she declared, straightening out her legs and surveying them.

To people who knew them, they were an unlikely

match. Bart, the architect, smart, precise, tidy – his favourite adage: a place for everything and everything in its place. His preferred time of year was the winter when the coldness sealed everyone into their homes, and the streets were like crisp sheets, pavements bleached and regularly swept clean. His preferred holiday destination would be to a place where the climate was cool, to a city where the architecture was of clean lines and the avenues were at right angles to one another, and where snow-capped mountains beckoned in the distance. Dorla, on the other hand, would choose the heat of a Mediterranean summer, a place where the heat rises in twisted plumes, sun-crisped leaves rattle in the trees, and the living scents and sounds of an ancient city fill the air. Neither would consider a vacation without the other as, despite their differences, they loved each other and enjoyed each other's company. So they strove to choose a place that would please them both – a place that would encompass both their desires.

Bart was studying the graphs of the weather for previous years: the rainfall, the temperature, and the hours of sunshine. All the statistics were displayed on the fridge and, like on most evenings, their dinner plates, cutlery and condiments were nestled among the travel books, a salt cellar perched on a hill of magazines like a triangulation point.

Finally, they agreed on their destination, and Bart had begun to draft the itinerary. He refused to fly anywhere on account of the restrictive leg room most airlines afforded their passengers. Timetables had to be consulted, train arrivals matched with bus departures, right down to how many minutes it would take to walk from point A to point B (taking into account the gradient and prevailing winds). Dorla left him to it. She would only feel annoyed and frustrated at him if she tried to intervene, and anyway she knew how much he enjoyed the organising aspect of the holiday. So, once the schedule was fixed, Bart began to draw up the equipment list. He planned for, and it seemed as if he thought of, every eventuality that time and place might require.

It was a sweltering August day when Bart and Dorla arrived at the small Bavarian town, having travelled across sea and land by public transport for three days and nights. Bart was disconcerted that his careful timetabling had not proved to be correct, and Dorla could not help but point out that a two-and-a-half-hour flight would have got them there without the discomforts they had endured. At least the itinerary allowed for a couple of days of rest on arrival.

On the first day, Bart had planned to visit the town hall. Dorla thought she would rather stay within the shady courtyard of the hotel, find a seat next to the fountain, and read her book. Later, she would set off to find the down town area where the flea markets engulfed the narrow streets.

'Why don't you come with me?' Bart asked. 'Honestly, there's nothing else like it.'

'But I've seen plenty of town halls,' she said. Wherever they went, they had to visit the civic buildings of each town.

'But this one is different,' said Bart. 'You'll see symmetry in action.'

'If it's in action, how can it remain symmetrical?'

'Time is action through the action of time,' Bart murmured. Or Dorla thought she heard something to that effect, but Bart was drifting off into his thoughts, so she decided not to ask him to explain further.

'I'll come along for a little while, and then I'll head off to the market. Let's meet up for lunch at one o'clock.'

The Neues Rathaus was a brand new building, not an old town hall at all, as she had imagined. It formed an unlikely companion, standing adjacent to the old town hall, and in stark contrast to its Gothic neighbour. It was built in a style that was considered progressive, according to Bart, in its *raison d'être* as well as its functionality. Dorla had visited many buildings since her life with Bart had begun, and thought of herself as well versed in architectural heritage; but to be fair, this one did not come into any category she had ever encountered. Dorla was looking at a building that was nothing other than a box that appeared to be squatting over an underground storage vault. It was plain, and it was simple, refreshing in its way, but it had none of the civic or religious iconographies of its older namesake, none of the historical expression or fine archaic detail that she so loved.

In preparation for their holiday, Bart had printed out the floor plan of the Neues Rathaus and studied the layout. It was exactly the building that he appreciated most, and he had had the foresight to book a personal tour of the entire hall and its cellars. He knew he would not be disappointed if it proved to be anything like how it was described: built with good-quality craftsmanship, high specifications, and with a simple yet clever construction; the ultimate design for one who revelled in neatness, straight lines, and immaculate systems.

Dorla entered the Neues Rathaus with a feeling of resignation and constraint. Inside the building was a lofty, pinewood, white-walled room where the light entered from the skylights and refracted identical rhomboid shapes onto a pale floor. Bart explained, in a hushed voice, that the height or the movement of the sun would not elongate or shorten the refractions, and there were no variations even once the midday point had passed. It was true that the hall looked the same whichever way one viewed it.

'Look up,' Bart said. 'Up at the windows. See how they move.'

Dorla studied the skylights; her neck strained until she felt she might fall over backwards. However hard she looked, there seemed to be no movement at all, but then she noticed something that was hardly visible; the glass was flowing like water on a calm lake, in slow, tiny shifts.

'They are following the direction of the sun,' Bart explained, 'thereby providing an equanimity of light. Can you feel the sense of stillness, of perfection?'

'Yes,' said Dorla, with just a hint of surprise in her voice.

'Well, don't be taken in by it,' Bart said. 'It is merely an illusion of symmetry.'

Dorla smiled and leaned into Bart; she kissed his neck.

'I'll leave you to your tour of the vault,' she said.

He smiled and touched her shoulder, but his eyes did not leave the ceiling.

Dorla set off towards the centre of the town. She passed a biergarten with long empty tables and benches, and a man who was sweeping the street outside a fast-food place. As she walked past, he spat onto the pavement. Further on, the street became busier. People were moving slowly, a dreamy look on their faces as they gazed all about them. Dorla looked into the shop windows at all the tacky goods of the souvenir industry: plastic flags displaying the Bavarian coat of arms, miniature cuckoo clocks, dolls dressed in lederhosen, edelweiss fridge magnets, and clocks with flashing lights. She noticed that the clocks were all set at the same time: 10.00 am.

A vulgar town, thought Dorla; all that wonderful history subsumed in a morass of blinking façades and neon signs. She soon tired, and the traffic fumes were giving her a headache. Dorla was desperate to be away from the incessant cars, the reversing delivery trucks, the hush of air brakes, the beeps of the pedestrian crossings.

She did not see it at first – the narrow alleyway between the blocks of renovated buildings. She slipped down the snicket and was relieved to find that the sounds of the street quickly faded. Now, she was alone on a walkway where the paving stones were chipped but shiny as if polished by regular footfall. The alleyway continued, becoming narrower and narrower until she thought it must soon come to an end, but, to her surprise, it turned at a ninety-degree angle and then it opened out.

She was standing at the edge of a town square in the old sector judging by the buildings. They had low-slung cantilevered floors that, if she had been an inch or two taller, would have clipped the top of her head. Dorla was standing under an arch of ornate ironwork. She wondered how old it was; difficult to tell, certainly a well-made replica. Bart would have known the date by the design of the buildings. He had told her that as a child he had loved castles, and he had learned all about them. All his pocket money had been spent on miniature bricks and mechanical parts for engineering; cogs and wheels and axles. He would reconstruct engines, buildings, palaces, drawbridges, moats – anything he saw in the history books. Dorla smiled as she thought about Bart. He had not changed much, only now his model-building was done under the guise of a professional career. He was an architect, paid to produce plans and models of buildings, and he was highly lauded for his work. His buildings were innovative, of the highest specifications, detailed but not decorative, and all worthy and effective. 'Detail the infinite, seek out perfection,' would be his leitmotif.

In front of her, the traders were shouting their wares; rustic tables creaked with produce. She could not understand what they were shouting, but it was Germanic – maybe a local dialect. Under her feet, the pith of citrus speckled the ground, loose cabbage leaves crunched, and apples rolled like pinballs along the gullies between the stalls, their flesh exposed and bruised. It was perfect. A re-enactment society's re-creation of a bustling Tudor or late medieval town.

Along to the left, the stalls were set with earthenware

pots, glassware, copperware, and a line of bone-handled knives. One stall was dedicated to lidded pots, and in front of it, there was a large container full of carved walking sticks. The next stall held hammers, nails, and horse shoes of different sizes. She picked up several items, but none seemed quite right for souvenirs; they were mostly heavy and utilitarian. Dorla wandered along enjoying the drifting pipe smoke and other scents, some sweet and ripe, some overripe, but all pierced with the aroma of spices: nutmeg, cinnamon, and coffee.

It was the aroma of coffee that brought Dorla back to the moment – the mid-morning moment when she would have liked to find a street café and indulge in the delights of *kaffee und kuchen*. With this in mind, she walked across the square, all the time dodging the barrow-handlers with their loaded carts. A carillon of bells began to strike single notes, and then to ring out in a cascade playing a tune that was at once familiar and strange. She walked towards the tower, fascinated by the wooden figurines that shuffled across the front of the glockenspiel clock. The peal of music stopped, and the clock struck once – only once. It did not make any sense if it was one o'clock already, not when she had left Bart at the Neues Rathaus at ten o'clock. Of that, she was certain. They had agreed to meet for lunch at one o'clock, and so she headed towards what she thought was the direction of the town hall. She hoped that Bart would be feeling satisfied with his morning tour – enough to go back to the hotel for lunch and an afternoon nap. She longed to have her feet rubbed. She kept on walking, a little distracted by her thoughts. She always appreciated Bart's attention to detail when it came to massaging.

The Rathaus was in front of her now. She felt relieved. She would walk in and surprise him. No doubt he would still be discussing the finer details of the building's construction with the tour guide. The old Rathaus was indeed beautiful; she couldn't help but admire its Gothic façade, but the frontage was obscured by the people on the steps of the grand entrance. Two men in grey tunics were haggling noisily, and there were cages of chickens piled one on top of another. There was even a goat tied to one of the pillars. A pig squealed so loudly that she put her hands over her ears – she thought it was being slaughtered. Surely not in the town square; that would be barbaric. This part of the show had not been organised very well – the stench would put anyone off. There seemed to be no consideration for health and safety. Dorla could appreciate that they had gone to a lot of trouble to bring the atmosphere of a medieval town to life, but she was beginning to feel disorientated, and irritated by the heat and the smell; she thought she might be sick. She slipped on the cobbles of the concourse. Her ankle stung with the twist, but she carried on; at least she was almost at the Neues Rathaus. Now it would only be a matter of a minutes before she was back with Bart.

But this was the old Rathaus; she had approached it from the other direction. How easily she had become lost. She set off to walk around to the other side to find the Neues Rathaus. She had felt sure that it was on the left-hand side of the old Rathaus, but she must have been mistaken. Hadn't she seen the plans enough times? In any case, she had walked away from the building just a short time ago.

Finally, she was at the far end of the marketplace. In this shaded area, the ground was soft and slippery, and her open sandals did not protect her from the detritus that lay everywhere. It was not the usual rubbish – paper cups, crisp packets, tickets, used tissues – but animal droppings, yellow streams of urine, and even a ruby liquid that could be real blood. The re-enactment, if that was what it was, had gone too far. Now she yearned to be back in the streamlined, straight-sided, clean world of Bart's Neues Rathaus, but, for some reason, it wasn't there. From here she could still hear the hubbub of the marketplace, but the further she went, the more it died away. Then, all was quiet; no sound of traffic, nothing but the distant chatter of voices, the odd grunts and snorts of animals.

She sat on a step, lowered her head onto her knees, closed her eyes and tried to think about her route: how she might have gone wrong. She stared at the cobbles between her feet, holding her hair in her fists. She felt angry, and she wanted to shout at someone, at Bart in particular. Whose stupid idea was it to come here? But whenever Dorla vented her frustration, Bart would wait for the storm to pass, hug her when she cried, and sometimes, later on, he would bring her a gift to ease her heart. It was never a gift of flowers bought from a supermarket, but some other token: a fine feather that had fallen from a dove-cote, the filigree remains of a holly leaf or a heart-shaped stone from a path of pebbles.

Queen of the Sea

I am so weary of their clamorous chatter, their irksome babble. I slip between the boulders and crouch as if to mesh a moment into rock. There I sigh and breathe within the privacy of my stone throne. Hearing the echoed cries of my advisors, I chuckle at their disarray, their panic, as they search the caves below the cliffs, while others wade through the slush-sand shallows. All the while, they are calling, calling.

Over the bladderwrack rocks, my feet press the popping sacs. I hunker for a while to watch the creatures in a rock pool: crabs, jellyfish, tiny sea urchins, dog whelks, winkles, limpets; all existing within the hierarchy of their private briny world. And yet these men, so astute (they believe), so sagacious; these men of courage, brain and brawn know less than a barnacle on a rock. They believe that I, Knut, have the power to halt the tide.

I shudder. Cold waves lash at my legs. I leap onto a dry rock, but before I can compose myself, I am exposed, ousted by the last rays of sun that sends out its jewel-studded streaks into the bronzing light.

My dearest Emma will, at this time, be sailing from the coast of Normandy. Her pilgrimage has been long, but her mission has been twofold. Not only has she sought to visit the shrine of Our Lady but, by my urging, she has secured the lands of her inheritance. But now, on her return, she must face her deepest fear again: the crossing of the sea.

❦

I lay on my couch as the ghost-mists of night descend, and I pray for deliverance from the task that awaits me with the silver daggers of dawn. Elevated on this mound of the dune, I watch the stars through a triangle of the canvas. I can just see the spray at the shoreline, how it is refracted in the slip-shine of the moon; how each wave delivers an epiphany of plight. My breath is held before each rumbling ebb, and there is fear in my heart. Each slap of every wave draws further on the silt, gnawing at the edge of my kingdom. How can my kingship be tested in this way? What greater warrior do they need? I am not almighty as some would have it. I know that my power on Earth goes by His grace alone. Only He commands the seas. I know too well the force of nature is not the territory of man, it never has been and never will be, not for anyone, neither peasant nor king.

Now, my subjects wish to secure a place for me among the Gods, or, perhaps, they simply seek to make a fool of me. They say I must command the seas; at my will, I am to turn the tide.

King. That is a mighty word. It is one that I own and will not easily relinquish. I am Knut, The Great: King of Denmark, Norway, England, some of Sweden too, an Emperor no less. I stand before the gates of Christendom, a mortal king, and this knowledge is my strength. Never have I believed that I could rule more than the land, not the birds in the sky, nor the fish in the sea. But my courtiers have no humility, and they are bent on testing my powers, my majesty.

Bardric, my loyal and trusted friend, came to me and spoke of this concern.

'They request that you command the tide,' says he.

I laugh. 'Then they have lingered too long in this country of green spirits, witchery, and fairy craft,' I reply. 'And you?'

'I am a fool, your Majesty, it's true,' he says, 'but a fool who listens with his heart.'

'So they have taken you for an idiot, Bardric,' I reply.

'Your Majesty, they will not leave the subject alone,' he continues, 'not until your greatness has been proven.'

'Surely you are not taken in by these foreign lords?' I cry. 'This piffle is a trap; it's set to undermine me.'

'There is talk, your Majesty...' he continues.

'Talk is talk! Is my power over many lands not proof enough that I am fit to be their king?'

'As their king, only you can decide.'

He is shrewd. There is no flicker of humour around his mouth.

'So, they wish for me to halt the course of the tide? Reverse its natural flow?'

Bardric nods his agreement.

'The sea is a force of nature tuned to the stars, the planets and the shifting winds,' I declare. 'It is far greater than a single man, even one who is a king.'

Bardric is silent.

So now, it has come to this. This challenge to my authority must be quelled. If I am to keep my crown, I must prove my worth without losing their loyalty, or, indeed, I will lose face. I cannot admit my fear.

I was never like my father. Sweyn Forkbeard held no fear of the sea. On my first expedition, I felt safe within the orbit of my father's eye. But we were drawn into the rough seas around the islands of Orkney in our narrow long-ship just as a storm began. In between the flashes of lightning, a mountain of the sea appeared, erupting before our eyes, its toppling edge tipping us onto our side as we clung on to the vessel, bound ourselves with ropes strapped to the hull, the masts, or to each other. Several men were lost. I believed we too would drown as we tilted against the maw of a deep whirlpool, but as we circled its outer ring, the force lessened, and, by divine intervention and with the might of those on board, we broke free of the jaws that threatened to swallow us.

Later, when I assembled my fleet, I insisted that only the best, the strongest, the fastest, should be employed. I declared my fleet invincible: 22 long, sturdy ships with sails for greater speed, 10,000 men equipped with armour, shields and oars, provisions to last a year at sea.

❧

Daybreak will bring the point of the lowest tide when the waxing of the seasons has reached its vernal peak; it is the time of Equinox. And it is also said by the gossip-mongers, that, at first light, I, King Knut, shall pit his power against the vastness of the world to claim the ultimate crown, King of the Seas.

For three moons now, the bards have sung their fine-teased lyrics, the jesters have provoked with their jocularity, the maids have tittle-tattled, the cooks have spread rumours, even my knights and squires speak of little else. The time has come to deal with this absurdity.

But still I do not know how it can be done, and I will not have the history books say that I was the fool who thought he could reverse the tide. No.

I look to heaven, but how does heaven look on me?

I call for my sword of iron, the metal that is drawn from

the earth, smelted in the pits of fire, hammered into a warrior's sword. My answer must surely lie in the blade that has saved me on countless times. My right hand is adept, used to the wielding of this implement, controlled by the deftness of my wrist.

I withdraw the crafted blade from its sheath, and as I do, a small item drops to the ground, and, for a moment, it is lost on the intricate woven carpet. My hand reaches out, feels for the floor around my feet.

I hold up the coin to the light. 'CNUT REX ANGLORU,' it reads.

One penny: a keepsake, the first coin cut by the minter in London, given to me for luck, a present from my beloved Emma, who, for all I know, is lost at sea – the vessel made unsafe, or damned with the blight of disease. We had word of the outward journey from travellers who have since returned. The Abbess, Emma's life-long companion, fell ill and died, and I know that the loss of her childhood friend to the sea will have caused her much distress. My poor Emma, who suffers so greatly from the sickness, a malady that affects even the sturdiest of sailors.

I look through the opening of the tent. My view is of our Royal Encampment and that portion of my kingdom's land within arm's length: a dune that is enclosed, canopied, hemmed by a ring of fluttering pennants. What invader lies beyond us?

Despite all precautions, the incident at Orkney haunts my darkest dreams. And now, at the cusp of night and day, I sweat as if with fever despite the stillness of the air. The haunting sounds of the sea enter my tent. The camp is suffused with the base light of dawn. The armour of an army glints: limbless breastplates, shields, helmets, all spark with the first risings of the sun as if in readiness for combat, or else to greet the King of the Sea.

I hear a beat, the drum of time. My heart, quickening and rising in my chest. My throat constricts. I will fail, fall ill, or fall from grace, just at the moment of my testing. Am I the one who dares demean His power? What right have I to pit myself against His grace? I will escape. But where can I go?

The beat of my heart is escalating until it is overtaken, soon replaced by another familiar sound, a welcome sound – the rhythm of hooves.

'Queen Emma arrives from France.' A servant's voice breaks the dawn like a fanfare that coincides with the full rising of the sun.

She is alive. Who but my beloved Emma knows better of the tempests of the sea? Who suffers more than her, whose fear is greater? And she, my brave queen, has sailed the stormy sea to her homeland on the Norman coast and returned safely. My dear, Emma. She is the Queen of the Sea. Now is not the time to tempt providence.

I hold the fine edge of my sword to the light, observe its sheen, how the silvering is just as it was the day it was drawn from the forger's fire.

I know what I must do.

'Set my chair above the line of the tide,' I command. 'Turn it to face the land.'

There is no Birdsong

Glen swings the car to the left, leaving the road for a track that is stony and potholed. He knows he should have carried on, but he doesn't relish the task ahead. The car jolts over the ruts, and once or twice the exhaust scrapes the ground. The heavy rainfall has washed away any semblance of a road surface, not that it had ever been more than a simple track running through the trees – a trail for the trucks carrying the stone from the quarry. Lately, the deciduous woods have been cleared and much of the surrounding land planted with pine trees. But somehow the lane seems shorter and narrower than Glen remembers. But then, he was only ten years old the last time. He was the small boy pointing towards the lake, with a policeman hunkered beside him asking him questions.

The trees are thinning out as he comes to the end of the track. He is almost there – but he stops, pressing hard on the brake. Gripping the steering wheel, he turns it sharp to the left. His knuckles are white. His forehead is beaded with sweat. The wheels spin as the car twists on its axis until it has turned a full one hundred and eighty degrees. He shoves the gearstick into first, then pulls it back into second. As he lets out the clutch, the car lurches forward, grinding on the gritty track. Once he is back on the main road, on the smooth tarmac, he drives on, slowing down for the final mile towards the house.

Glen knows he must focus on what must do today. He knows the past is another country, another lifetime, and he intends to be methodical, to work his way through each room, gathering up their belongings, sorting them into piles ready for the house clearance company who will arrive tomorrow. He can't bear the thought of strangers sifting through his family's possessions, but he is determined that he will keep nothing. This is the home of his childhood, that first decade of simplicity they existed as a perfect family: him, his parents, and his sister, Laura.

First things first; Glen opens the larder door and reaches into the depths until his fingers find the bottle. It is dusty, having lain on its side since last Christmas, or maybe the Christmas before. He is relieved that it still contains some of its liquor. He places a glass on the table and pulls out the old cork with his thumbs. All around is all the dusty evidence of his parents' saddened lives. A sister would know what to do, what should be kept for posterity, which things to disregard. But it shouldn't be just down to him. The prickle of disbelief, of old anger, rises on the back of his neck.

Once fortified, this feeling of abandonment is temporarily banished. Glen sets to work: emptying cupboards and shelves, releasing the cabinets of their pungent medications, clearing the mantelpiece of ornaments. He lifts the paintings and framed prints from their fixings and takes them into the hallway. He puts them down on the floor, their images facing the wall. He is satisfied with the progress he is making. By midday, all that is left is the oak chest of drawers in the living room. He takes a bin bag and shakes it open in readiness to fill it with the contents.

The top drawer is stiff, but, with a little effort, it shuffles open. It is stuffed with papers, envelopes, old cards, ribbons, things collected over half a century or more. They 'might come in useful one day', he hears his mother saying. His knuckles catch against the wooden frame, and he swears, feeling guilty as if she might still hear him. The contents are old letters, a housekeeper's notebook filled with the handwriting of archaic loops and the words of domesticity: tea, a pint of milk, 1lb tripe. There are birthday cards, recipes torn from magazines, a ball of elastic bands – and a pair of clippers. He runs his hand over his balding head, remembering the stubble left in their wake, the sudden chill around his young ears.

There is a large brown envelope at the bottom of the drawer. It is unsealed, and as Glen lifts it out the photographs spill before him. There is his father standing by the gate of the house – this house, even the same gate. His father is wearing a soldier's uniform; an army cap placed squarely on his head. There's another of a carthorse attached to a single plough, its neck and shoulders flexed as if straining to drag its burden through the clods of clay. Glen recognises the plough. It is still in the tin-roofed shed in the yard, its prongs flaking with rust, tines eroded, orange stains tinting the earthen floor. There is a photograph of his father, this time as a child, standing in front of a cart filled high with hay and there's a girl next to him, Glen's aunt, the one he never met. He only knows that she was called Laura too. In others, the images are burnished and faded into sepia shadows, ghostly evidence of another time.

Then he sees the photograph of his mother as a girl. It is quite uncanny: she looks so much like his sister, the same high cheekbones, the same eyes gazing into an unknowable future. There's a date written in white at the bottom right-hand corner. He works it out – she was twelve years old, twelve years before she had her first child, Laura. As his eyes water, the face in the photo recedes, becoming blurred, hardly visible.

Glen rushes outside, leaving a trail of papers in his wake and the invisible footprints of grief. He is outside in the little yard at the back of the house. Behind him, the building is echoing with the voices of the dead, his memories and theirs. At least the garden is alive with the sound of the birds in the trees and the lightness of the scents in the air. Glen breathes in, filling his whole body, holding his breath for a moment before letting it go. He places his hand on the wall, feeling the steady rock beneath him, for a moment absorbing its solidity.

❧

Every day, after school, Glen would go straight to his bedroom, and there he'd wait for Laura. She was three years older and at a different school. But she was always kind to her young brother. She had her reasons, and he understood that, even then, but any kindness was better than none. In return, he was the keeper of her secrets, the witness of her actions. At night, when the house was quiet and their parents slept, Laura would climb out of the window, onto the roof of the kitchen extension, and slip quietly onto the damp ground by the broken drainpipe. Through the window Glen watched Laura running up the lane towards the forbidden lake, the deep lagoon that was formed from the cuttings of the old quarry. There was an opening at one end and a shelf of land that sloped down to the edge of the water. On the far side, the slag heap of rocky spoils had been cordoned off with a roll of barbed wire. There had been slippages in the past, and there were signs all around, their painted words declared that here was a place of danger, that cold water kills. Laura was not deterred as she slipped into the icy pool, and swam as hard as she could across the breadth of the lake as far as the overhang on the other side. She wanted to be the fastest swimmer in her school, in the district. She wanted to beat the record, to win the county medal.

It was during the half term holiday when Laura persuaded Glen to go with her. The sun was burning its last embers, its orange flames reflecting on the surface of the lake. This time, Laura was intent on swimming its full length, as far as the reed banks on the other side. A small stream fed its dark spills into the clear water beyond where the whirlpools bubbled, fed by the subterranean springs. The sheer-sided quarried rocks allowed no purchase; the depth was unknown – it was said that underneath there were cracks, openings to a bottomless chasm. Laura had worked out that if she swam from end to end twenty-five times, she would have completed a full mile, but she needed Glen to record the time it took. That evening, they stood silently together, watching the water as it shimmered innocently in the glowing light of the early summer air. There were large gnats playing on the surface, and fireflies flickering in the trees.

❦

Glen still has the bottom drawer to empty, the one that is marked with tiny teeth marks from the mice that run rampant behind the fittings and skirting boards of the house. Glen shakes and tips the contents into the bin, letting the rodent droppings roll away. There are several newspapers, and they are folded neatly and tied together with string. They are faded and have yellowed with age. Glen pulls at the string to release them. Some are so fragile they disintegrate, exuding a dusty pungency that eviscerates the air. He recognises the local paper of his childhood, *The*

Daily Chronicle. It was always delivered to the house late in the afternoons, and snatched up by his father who would spend the next hour reading it while Mother prepared the evening meal. The only time his father looked up was to comment on an article or dismiss the complaints of the letters page, but mainly to remark on the stupidity of others.

There was one dated Saturday, 29th May, 1976. The front page has been torn out, separated from the rest of the papers, which remain complete. Glen brushes the back of his hand across the newsprint: 'Swimming for Gold' is the headline, and underneath the photograph: 'Aspiring Olympic Swimmer, Laura Ashton, 13'. Laura is on a diving board with her arms stretched up; her head tucked in. She is looking down, measuring the gap, the distance of air between the board and the water of the swimming pool. Beside it is another image of Laura holding a certificate, with a bold, confident look, her mouthed stretched into a smile.

There is one more item at the back of the drawer: a tiny black tote bag. Glen picks it up hardly looking, but closing his fist around it. For a moment he is back at the lake. He wishes he had refused to go there that evening. Perhaps, then, she would not have been tempted to swim to the far end, to the place where the whirling pools sucked her into the deep. He wishes the next day had not followed the night, the night of the search, or that the morning had never arrived with its emptiness.

With the car now full of boxes and bags, Glen drives away, turning off again at the track. This time he goes all the way to the end. He gets out, shuts the car door and walks to the edge, towards the shelf of land, the narrow piece of ground sloping down to the place where Laura entered the water – only now it is covered with gorse and bracken.

Everything is the same, yet different. The lake, the blue lagoon of Glen's memory, is now a cloudy grey pool. There is a pall of mist moving towards him from the other side in wispy fingers rising above the edge, reaching into the trees. The lake is shrouded in silence.

There is no birdsong.

Glen is standing on a rock above the sandy shelf that dips into the water. He takes out the stopwatch from the tote bag. He feels the weight of its cold metal in his hand. He looks up and sees the splash of water: a fish leaps up, twisting in the air, then it disappears below the surface leaving a circle of ripples that overlap and finally diminish. He presses the button of the stopwatch. The numbers begin to turn, clicking second by second. He presses it again. How he wishes he could halt the time, that time could be suspended by the push of a button.

He is watching his sister as she swims across the lake towards the dark of the overhang. 'Laura!' he cries, but his voice echoes back at him, swallowed in the distance, a lonely child's voice, unanswered.

Saving Grace

On the market stall is a box formed in the style of a Swiss chalet. The name embossed on the lid is Grace. When I lift the roof, a ballerina emerges and twirls to the sound of tinkling music. The stall holder smiles and holds up five fingers to denote the price. I am transfixed by the tiny dancer: her silk dress is grubby and stained, and the hair that would once have been held up in a neat pleat is now loose and dishevelled. She looks so tired, and as I cup my hand around her, I feel the motion of the spin and realise that she has very little energy. The twirling slows to a halt.

The stall holder is serving another customer as the music stops. I snap the dancer off her plinth. I close the music box, and I walk away. I am not sure why I do this. Now, inside my pocket is a tiny ballerina – one that belongs inside a music box whose life has always been at the mercy of the turning of the key that winds the coil which in turn sets off the mechanism that causes the dancer to rotate.

When I look back, I see that the merchant is talking to another customer and that the box remains closed on the table. I continue walking through the market, looking at the other stalls. I have almost forgotten about my act of vandalism when I push my hand into my pocket for the coins to pay for a kilo of oranges.

I feel a movement under my hand, a slight buzz, and the brush of silken material against my palm. I feel a twinge, a niggle of guilt. I have stolen a ballerina, and now she is imprisoned within the dark lining of my coat.

The next stall along from the greengrocer's has a display of wooden bird boxes. They look just like real houses, with painted windows and chimney pots, and they stand high above the ground on their platforms. I linger, and as I withdraw my hand from my pocket, I glance around to see if anyone is watching. I pop the dancer into the entrance hole of a nesting box. It has a ladder, so she will be able to come and go as she pleases, and there is no music to make her spin on her points or make her hair fly across her face.

She will no longer be made to turn around and around.

Acknowledgements

Some of these stories have won prizes or been previously published. I'd like to thank the competition judges, and the editors of the following reviews and magazines:

Halo Literary Magazine (issue 2, 2017) – Wink.

The London Magazine (June 2015, online). Winner of 3rd prize, *The London Magazine* competition 2015 – Into the Blue.

Litro (October 2015, online) – A Witness of Waxwings.

14th International Conference for the Short Story in English 2016, Shanghai, short story contest, 3rd Prize winner – Sea Level.

Visual Verse (vol. 1, ch. 1, online) – Carapace.

Junoesq (August 2015) – Clock, Time, Stop.

The Lampeter Review (issue 13, 2016) – Beast Market (Viridescence).

Deep Water Literary Journal (February 2014) – Mother Tongue.

Firewords (Issue 4) – Sprite.

Lakeview International Journal of Literature and Arts (2016) – A Taste for Blood.

Halo Literary Magazine (issue 2, 2017) – Gestation.

All the Sins (2017) – Intercession.

Shortlisted for the Strands International 'Fire' competition – The Dissonance (The Bells of St Ronan).

The Copperfield Review (2014) – Queen of the Sea (The Fear of King Cnut).

Long-listed for the Strands International 'Water' competition, 2017 – There is no Birdsong.

Commended by Paper Swans Press (August 2015)– Saving Grace (Dancing Free).

Cultured Llama Publishing
Poems | Stories | Curious Things

Cultured Llama was born in a converted stable. This creature of humble birth drank greedily from the creative source of the poets, writers, artists and musicians that visited, and soon the llama fulfilled the destiny of its given name.

Cultured Llama aspires to quality from the first creative thought through to the finished product.

www.culturedllama.co.uk

Also published by Cultured Llama

Poetry

strange fruits by Maria C. McCarthy
Paperback; 72pp; 203×127mm; 978-0-9568921-0-2; July 2011

A Radiance by Bethany W. Pope
Paperback; 70pp; 203×127mm; 978-0-9568921-3-3; June 2012

The Night My Sister Went to Hollywood by Hilda Sheehan
Paperback; 82pp; 203×127mm; 978-0-9568921-8-8; March 2013

Notes from a Bright Field by Rose Cook
Paperback; 104pp; 203×127mm; 978-0-9568921-9-5; July 2013

The Fire in Me Now by Michael Curtis
Paperback; 90pp; 203×127mm; 978-0-9926485-4-1; August 2014

Cold Light of Morning by Julian Colton
Paperback; 90pp; 203×127mm; 978-0-9926485-7-2; March 2015

Zygote Poems by Richard Thomas
Paperback; 66pp; 178×127mm; 978-0-9932119-5-9; July 2015

Les Animots: A Human Bestiary by Gordon Meade, images by Douglas Robertson
Hardback; 166pp; 203×127mm; 978-0-9926485-9-6; December 2015

Memorandum: Poems for the Fallen by Vanessa Gebbie
Paperback; 90pp; 203×127mm; 978-0-9932119-4-2; February 2016

The Light Box by Rosie Jackson
Paperback; 108pp; 203×127mm; 978-0-9932119-7-3; March 2016

There Are No Foreign Lands by Mark Holihan
Paperback; 96pp; 203×127mm; 978-0-9932119-8-0; June 2016

After Hours by David Cooke
Paperback; 92pp; 203×127mm; 978-0-9957381-0-2; April 2017

There Are Boats on the Orchard by Maria C. McCarthy
Paperback; 36pp; 210×115mm; July 2017

Hearth by Rose Cook
Paperback; 120pp; 203×127mm; 978-0-9957381-4-0; September 2017

The Year of the Crab by Gordon Meade
Paperback; 88pp; 203×127mm; 978-0-9957381-3-3; October 2017

Short stories

Canterbury Tales on a Cockcrow Morning by Maggie Harris
Paperback; 138pp; 203×127mm; 978-0-9568921-6-4; September 2012

As Long as it Takes by Maria C. McCarthy
Paperback; 168pp; 203×127mm; 978-0-9926485-1-0; February 2014

In Margate by Lunchtime by Maggie Harris
Paperback; 204pp; 203×127mm; 978-0-9926485-3-4; February 2015

The Lost of Syros by Emma Timpany
Paperback; 128pp; 203×127mm; 978-0-9932119-2-8; July 2015

Only the Visible Can Vanish by Anna Maconochie
Paperback; 158pp; 203×127mm; 978-0-9932119-9-7; September 2016

Who Killed Emil Kreisler? by Nigel Jarrett
Paperback; 208pp; 203×127mm; 978-0-9568921-1-9; November 2016

A Short History of Synchronised Breathing and other stories by Vanessa Gebbie
Paperback; 132pp; 203×127mm; 978-0-9568921-2-6; February 2017

In the Wild Wood by Frances Gapper
Paperback; 212pp; 203×127mm; 978-0-9957381-6-4; June 2017

Curious things

Digging Up Paradise: Potatoes, People and Poetry in the Garden of England by Sarah Salway
Paperback; 164pp; 203×203mm; 978-0-9926485-6-5; June 2014

Punk Rock People Management: A No-Nonsense Guide to Hiring, Inspiring and Firing Staff by Peter Cook
Paperback; 40pp; 210×148mm; 978-0-9932119-0-4; February 2015

Do it Yourself: A History of Music in Medway by Stephen H. Morris
Paperback; 504pp; 229×152mm; 978-0-9926485-2-7; April 2015

The Music of Business: Business Excellence Fused with Music by Peter Cook
Paperback; 318pp; 210×148mm; 978-0-9932119-1-1; May 2015

The Hungry Writer by Lynne Rees
Paperback; 246pp; 244×170mm; 978-0-9932119-3-5; September 2015

Lightning Source UK Ltd.
Milton Keynes UK
UKOW04f2232171217
314655UK00001B/39/P